'You are so voice wash... gasped as ... across her ~~parted lips. But we~~ can't.'

His words took a few microseconds to penetrate the haze surrounding her mind. 'Stephen?'

He swallowed and, after exhaling harshly, dropped his hand and pulled back. 'Nicolette…I care about you, you must realise that.'

'And I care about you.'

'But we've both been hurt in the past, and come Monday…' He trailed off.

'Come Monday we'll be working together,' she finished for him, her eyes stinging with tears. She cleared her throat, trying to get control over her voice. 'I know.'

Dear Reader

My husband and I spent part of our honeymoon in the Blue Mountains, which are part of the Great Dividing Range. Stephen and Nicolette's story is based around Blackheath—the town where we stayed on our honeymoon.

We recently visited the area and fell in love with the untouched, natural beauty all over again. We also had the most amazing meal at the Megalong Tearooms, so I just had to include that in the book, too.

I thought this was the perfect setting for both Stephen and Nicolette to come to terms with their pasts so they could both finally move forward into the future—the future they end up sharing together.

I hope you enjoy **Crisis at Katoomba Hospital**.

With warmest regards,

Lucy Clark

BLUE MOUNTAINS A&E
Finding love in the most beautiful place of all.

Look out for the next story set in BLUE MOUNTAINS A&E featuring Stephen's twin coming soon from Mills & Boon® Medical Romance™.

Recent titles by the same author:

DIAGNOSIS: AMNESIA
UNDERCOVER DOCTOR
DR CUSACK'S SECRET SON

CRISIS AT KATOOMBA HOSPITAL

BY
LUCY CLARK

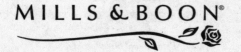

To Ruth—the best mother-in-law.
Thank you for always loving my work.
Rest peacefully.
Psalm 100.

All the characters in this book have no existence outside the imagination of the author, and have no relation whatsoever to anyone bearing the same name or names. They are not even distantly inspired by any individual known or unknown to the author, and all the incidents are pure invention.

First published in Great Britain 2005
Harlequin Mills & Boon Limited,
Eton House, 18-24 Paradise Road, Richmond, Surrey TW9 1SR

© Lucy Clark 2005

ISBN 0 263 84310 6

Set in Times Roman 10½ on 12 pt.
03-0605-47336

Printed and bound in Spain
by Litografia Rosés, S.A., Barcelona

CHAPTER ONE

'HELLO! Stephen?'

'Are you sure this is OK?' Nicolette whispered as her friend pushed open the door a little further.

'Of course. I'm his *sister*.' Stephanie walked in with confidence. 'Sisters are allowed to annoy their brothers when they're renovating, especially when he's not expecting it. Ooh. Good song. I like this one.'

Nicolette tried to listen to the words but all she heard, or felt rather, was the loud bass reverberating through the run-down house. 'Does he always have loud music on?' She raised her voice as they drew closer to the music.

'Only when he's creating.' Stephanie waved her arms flamboyantly in the air.

'I thought he was renovating.' Nicolette stepped carefully over a paint can, being careful not to get any on her shoes or trousers.

'Stephen?' his sister called again. 'Yoo-hoo.'

'Steph?' The deep reply came from the back room of the house. A second later, the music was cut and silence prevailed. 'Steph?'

'*C'est moi.* Is it safe to come through?' They continued picking their way through the rubble on the floor. Tools, ladders, buckets, dropsheets and painting rags.

His deep rich chuckle filled the silence and Nicolette felt goose bumps tickle her at the sound. Whoever Stephanie's brother was, he had a nice laugh.

'It was safe, but now you're here, who knows what might happen?'

'Hey,' she protested. 'Be nice. I brought a friend.'

'Really?'

In the next instant he appeared, and Nicolette found it hard not to suck in a breath. He was tall, dark and handsome—even though he was wearing a pair of faded denim jeans and an old T-shirt that were both splattered with paint, they certainly highlighted the perfect body beneath.

Stephen's gaze swept quickly over her, taking in her neat suit and swept-back blonde hair. She had deep brown eyes and the combination of light hair and dark eyes had him mesmerised for a second. He quickly recovered. 'Hello. I'm Stephen. I won't shake hands because I don't want to risk getting paint on you.'

Nicolette wasn't sure exactly how she'd lost control of her senses, whether it was his deep voice or hypnotic gaze which was still smouldering from his mirth, but she pasted on a smile. 'Thanks for the thought. I'm Nicolette.'

'Nic's the doctor I told you about,' Stephanie interjected. 'She's currently working at Dr River's practice, which is the one you'll be sort of taking over.'

Stephen merely nodded as his sister repeated information he already knew. He found it hard to pull his gaze away from the blonde doctor as Stephanie continued talking, but eventually he looked at his sister.

'To what do I owe the pleasure of this visit?'

'I brought your inaugural hospital roster. You're on tomorrow night.' She held out a piece of paper to him.

'Gee, thanks.' He studied the roster a moment before handing it back to Stephanie. 'Put it in the kitchen, please.'

'Also, I thought I'd give you a hand.'

Stephen raised his eyebrows as he took in his sister's neat work clothes. 'You're hardly dressed for it, little sister.'

'Oh, cut the "little", will you?' She turned to Nicolette. 'Just because he's a whole five minutes older than me, he thinks that makes him my *big* brother.'

'It does.'

'You're *twins*?'

'We're not identical,' Stephen said, deadpan. He jerked his thumb over his shoulder, indicating the room. 'I'm almost finished and I need to keep a wet edge, so if you don't mind I'd like to keep going.'

'Go ahead,' Stephanie answered and then said in an undertone, 'He's such a perfectionist.' In her normal tone she continued, 'I'll make us all a cuppa.' She headed off to the kitchen.

'That's OK.' Nicolette needed to go. The best way to get her heart rate back to normal was to get out of Stephen's presence as soon as possible. 'I'd better get going. It was nice to meet you, Stephen.' She poked her head into the room he was painting, the fumes assailing her senses.

'There's no need to rush off,' he said, his back to her as he rolled paint onto the wall. 'What do you think of the colour?'

'It's...soothing.'

'I take it you mean dull. It's called mushroom and it is quite bland, but I'm planning to do a faint border around the cornice which will add a touch of colour, and once the furnishings are in, the walls will complement everything. Besides, this is supposed to be a consulting room so I don't want it to be too overpowering for the patients.'

'You can see the whole picture?'

'He always can,' Stephanie answered for him as she returned. 'It's a gift I didn't get.'

'You have others, Steph.' He finished rolling the wall

and carefully placed his roller back into the tray before stepping back to survey his handiwork.

'You should see some of his paintings, Nic. They're amazing.'

'They're average,' Stephen corrected, turning to face his sister. 'Don't exaggerate, Steph. Besides, painting is personal. I don't do it for approval.' His face was serious with a small frown.

'Do you have some here?'

'No.'

'What do you do with them?' Nicolette asked, watching him closely. She'd seen that look before—on him—which was ridiculous. She'd only just met him. She gave herself a mental shake. She'd probably seen the look on Stephanie and now that they were standing side by side, she could see the strong resemblance between the two.

Both had the same shape and colour eyes, their noses were identical and so was the shape of their chins. She was also sure that Stephanie's natural colour was the same dark brown as her brother's, rather than the reddish gold it currently was. Also, Stephen didn't have an earring in sight, whereas Stephanie had at least four on each side.

'I have most of them in storage at the moment.'

'He's going to hang them all over this place,' Stephanie insisted firmly, and Stephen shook his head. 'He's been waiting a long time for his own practice and now he finally has it.' She leaned up and kissed his cheek. 'I'm just so glad you're finally here.'

'Where did you move here from?' Again Nicolette had the feeling she'd met him before, but she knew it was ridiculous. If she'd met this man before, she would certainly have remembered.

'Overseas.'

'I've been bugging him for the last twelve months to

come here. I mean, where else can you truly relax than here in the Blue Mountains? The scenery is the best, the people are even better and—'

'And *you're* in Katoomba whilst I'm in Blackheath,' Stephen finished for her. 'A whole fifteen minutes away.' His eyes twinkled mischievously. 'Close enough but not too close to prying, nosy little sisters.'

Stephanie gave him a playful punch in the stomach. 'Hey.' She laughed before saying, 'Ooh, that's the kettle. Tea or coffee, Nic?'

'Uh, none for me. I really should go. It was nice meeting you, Stephen.'

'Likewise.' He walked with her, leaving Stephanie to make the tea.

'You don't have to walk me out,' she protested as he came outside with her.

'Good excuse to get some fresh air.'

On the steps of the old house she turned to face him. 'Have we met before?'

Stephen took his time answering, looking at her intently. If he'd met this stunning woman before, he knew he'd have remembered. Even though the past few years of his life had been full of darkness, he definitely wouldn't have forgotten her. She was like a bright shining beacon. 'No.'

'Are you sure? You seem…familiar. Ever been to France?'

'Yes.'

'When?'

'Three years ago.'

'London?'

The frown creased his forehead again, as she'd seen before. 'I left just over twelve months ago. Nicolette, trust me, we haven't met before today.' The frown disappeared. 'How long have you known Stephanie?'

'About six months.'

'You've probably seen a photograph of me at her house or something like that.'

Nicolette shrugged. 'Never mind. It's probably the paint fumes getting to me, too.' She smiled politely and headed to her car. 'I'll see you tomorrow.'

'Tomorrow?'

'At the hospital. We're rostered on together.'

He nodded. 'See you then.' Stephen waited while she walked around to the driver's side of her old car. 'Drive safely.'

'I don't have far to go,' she said as she opened the door. 'I live two streets that way.' She pointed in the direction. 'Bye.'

Stephen waited and waved as she drove off, sucking a deep breath of fresh mountain air into his lungs before heading back inside. He walked to the kitchen and picked up the cup of tea his sister had made for him.

'Why did you bring Nicolette around?'

Stephanie grinned. 'Why? Do you like her?'

'She's attractive,' he acknowledged without inflection.

'She wanted to meet you.'

'Because?'

'Because she wants the security of a job when old man River sells out to you. Look, you need another GP when your practice opens and she needs a job. Also, then you'll have both a male and female doctor in the practice. It's a win-win situation.'

'Hmm.' He sipped his tea. 'How's the hospital?'

'Good.'

'Enjoying being top dog of the trauma unit?'

'Acting top dog, and I hate drawing up rosters. I'm a

doctor, not a magician. Everyone's always requesting certain days off or wanting to change.'

'I didn't.'

She smiled. 'You're not allowed to complain.'

'And why not?'

'Because you're scared of me.'

'Right.' He drawled the word slowly, his voice radiating pure disbelief. 'When does the new boss start?'

'Couple more weeks. He was supposed to be here next week but he's been held up, which means I have to do the rosters again.'

'Apart from the rosters?'

'I don't mind it.'

'You love it and you want it for your own.'

'Hey—get out of my head.'

'Too late, *little* sis.' Stephen sidestepped the swipe she took at him. 'I'm the one person in the world you just can't fool. Now, did you say you were here to help me or not?' He wanted to quiz her about Nicolette, to find out everything Stephanie knew about her, but at the same time he didn't want to know. He was here to unwind from the past few years, to spend time with his sister and to fulfil his dream of owning his own practice. The last thing he needed was a romantic entanglement with a blonde bombshell.

'Dr Brooks?'

'Yes.' Stephen turned to face the nursing sister who'd addressed him, one hand tightening around the handle of his briefcase.

She smiled. 'You look a little lost. Stephanie told me to look out for you.' She held out her hand. 'I'm Sophie and I'm the triage sister on duty tonight.'

Stephen shook her hand firmly before letting it go.

'Come this way.' Sophie led him down a corridor. 'Have you been here before?'

'To the Blue Mountains or to the hospital?'

'Both.'

'Blue Mountains once—when I was a child—and this is my first time in the hospital.'

'Well, you're bound to get lost. If that happens, grab a house phone and ask for directions.' She chuckled as they stopped outside a door. 'Male changing rooms. Females are just down the corridor. The code is 2605.'

He nodded, acknowledging her words.

'There should be plenty of vacant lockers—keys are in them so just pick one.'

'Thank you.'

'I'll see you back on the floor when you're ready.' Sophie smiled and headed back the way she'd come. Stephen turned and punched in the number she'd given him. It didn't work. He tried it again. Another error message. He frowned.

'Problem?'

Stephen turned to find Nicolette walking towards him. 'Yes.'

She stopped just short of him and looked him over. 'You're looking a bit more respectable. I almost didn't recognise you.' He was dressed in a navy suit, crisp white shirt and striped tie. Not a hair was out of place on his head and his black briefcase was clutched firmly in his hand. Very different from yesterday.

'Dr Stephen Brooks.' Stephen held out his free hand to her. 'Pleased to meet you Dr…' He frowned. 'I don't think Stephanie told me your last name.'

'Bourgeois.' Nicolette supplied absently as she scrutinised his hand. 'It's French.'

'So I gathered.'

'Any paint?' She gestured to his hand.

'I certainly hope not.'

Nicolette hadn't been able to stop thinking about him since they'd met late yesterday afternoon, and even though she kept telling herself it was because she was trying to figure out where she knew him from, in truth it was because he was an extremely good-looking man whom she'd been instantly attracted to. Then again, she'd been attracted to good-looking men before and it had only ended in heartbreak, so she'd told herself that this one was no different and she would do well not to waste her time on him. That little spiel had played itself over and over throughout the night and into the morning hours.

She'd been a little apprehensive about doing her hospital shift with him tonight, but she wasn't sure why. He was just a colleague. That's all. Nothing more. The instant she put her hand into his, she knew she was wrong.

Nicolette smothered her gasp at the instant warmth from his hand with a small cough and quickly withdrew. The after-effects continued to wreak havoc as tingles spread up her arm and flooded her entire body.

'Uh…' She cleared her throat, desperately trying to get her thoughts back on track. 'What code did Sophie give you?'

'Two-six-oh-five.'

She smiled. 'That's for the female changing rooms.'

'I doubt that will do me much good.' His tone was droll and although his eyes twinkled with a touch of humour, he didn't smile.

'You never know. Try 1702.'

'An easier code to remember.'

'Why?'

'It's my birth date.'

'Oh.' She nodded, then added, 'And Stephanie's, too, then.'

'That's what makes us twins.' He entered the code and was rewarded with a buzzing noise and then a click. He pushed on the door...and it worked.

'Open Sesame,' Nicolette said.

'Thank you.'

'You're welcome.' She waited for him to go through before she headed down the corridor to the female changing rooms. After she'd stowed her bag in her locker, she sat on a chair and forced herself to stop and think rationally. If she'd thought he was devastating with paint all over him, it was nothing compared to how he looked in a suit. Part of her had expected him to turn up to work as haphazardly dressed as he'd been yesterday, but another part of her had known with conviction that he'd wear a suit and look meticulous. Again, she searched her memory banks but came up blank.

Standing up, she attempted to push all thoughts of Stephen Brooks aside. 'Easier said than done,' she mumbled as she headed out to Accident and Emergency. How was she supposed to put him out of her mind when she'd be working with him for the next six hours?

He was already standing at the nurses' station with Sophie, getting the run-down on triage procedures. His jacket had been shed and he was in the process of meticulously rolling up his shirtsleeves to just below the elbow.

The buzzer for one of the examination cubicles went and Sophie headed off to answer it. Stephen turned and saw Nicolette. 'How many times a week do you work here?'

'Usually two—three if they're pushed. Depends on how much Stephanie can twist my arm.'

'Something she's well qualified at, believe me.' His

blue eyes were expressive as he spoke but he didn't smile. 'And how was your clinic today? Fairly busy?'

'No. Actually, this afternoon was quite slow.' She leant back against the desk, smoothing her hand down her brown skirt.

'Is it generally frantic?'

'Worried the patient base you're taking over could dwindle to nothing?'

'It's a consideration.'

Nicolette was once again struck with a sense of *déjà vu* as she looked at him, her mind trying to place where she'd seen him.

'We haven't met, Nicolette,' Stephen drawled, reading her mind.

'What?'

'You're mind is working at a frantic pace, trying to figure out where you've seen me before.' He shrugged nonchalantly. 'Trust me. I'd remember.'

'It's driving me nuts. I *know* I've seen you somewhere before. I have a clear picture of you in my mind.'

'There are plenty of places we could have crossed paths. Medical conferences, mutual friends or even just wandering around Portabello Market.'

'You liked to go there?'

'Yes.'

Sophie returned and looked at them both. 'Have either of you seen Stephanie?'

'No,' Nicolette answered for them both. 'Is she around?'

'She was about to leave when I saw her about half an hour ago, but I'm not sure whether she's actually managed to get out of here.'

'I hope she's gone. She worked an early shift,' Stephen said. Both women looked at him and he shrugged. 'She spent the night at my place and left very early this morning.'

'There was a lot of fog last night,' Sophie said.

'I'm amazed at how quickly it rolls in. I wouldn't let her go, even though she said she was used to driving in it.'

'The over-protective big brother?' Nicolette smiled at the thought, thinking of her own over-protective big brothers.

'Yes.' He paused for a moment, then a small smirk twitched at his lips. 'Drives her crazy.'

Sophie laughed. 'So naturally you do it. All right. Let me give you the run-down on what's happening here.' She preceded to tell them about their current patients and hand over the casenotes of the few patients still in the waiting room. 'Here's a file for you.' She held one out to Nicolette. 'And one for you.' She held the other out to Stephen. 'Welcome to Katoomba hospital.'

Stephen nodded his thanks and began reading the casenotes. He'd been quite happy to simply stand there all night and chat with Nicolette so actually doing some work was probably a good thing. As they were about to go call patients through, two of the nurses finished with their patients and walked wearily to the nurses' station.

'Let the night roll on,' one of them sighed and then straightened a little when she looked at Stephen, devouring him instantly with her gaze. 'Hello. I'm Lauren.' She held out her hand to him and Stephen shook it firmly.

'Stephen,' was all he said. He knew the bubbly brunette was flirting with him but he tried to ignore it. He was, for some reason, also highly conscious of the way Nicolette was watching him interact with the nurse. The urge to tell her the perky nurse wasn't his type surprised him. He didn't have to explain himself to anyone.

'And I'm Jade.' The other nurse smiled politely but continued with her work. 'Who's got Louise Briggs?' she asked them, pointing to the casenotes they held.

'I do,' Nicolette answered.

'She's in Examination Cubicle 2. Stephen, that means you have Mr Cole who's in EC-9.'

'I'll go with Stephen,' Lauren said quickly, and smiled brightly at him.

Stephen nodded briskly and headed off, Lauren trailing behind him.

'I hope he can cope,' Jade mumbled.

'I hear he's quite a brilliant doctor,' Nicolette responded as the two of them headed to EC-2.

'I don't mean medically. Lauren's like a piranha.'

Nicolette smiled. 'I think he can cope.' At least, she hoped he could. Did he fancy the young brunette? He hadn't shown any outward signs of accepting her attempts at flirting, but from the little she knew of him he was a man who gave nothing away with his facial expressions. She shook her head and sighed, shoving thoughts of him roughly aside as she pushed open the curtain of EC-2.

'Louise, I'm Dr Nicolette Bourgeois.' She smiled politely at her patient, who was lying on the examination bed with her right foot bandaged. 'It looks as though you've been having some fun. Jade, would you mind removing the bandage for me, please?' Nicolette scanned the notes. 'It says here you have some glass in your foot. How did that happen?'

'Dropped a glass and thought I'd vacuumed it all up but apparently not. I stood on a piece and managed to pull it out, but there was a lot of blood and I get kind of queasy…'

'You can say that again,' her husband, who was standing beside her holding her hand, chimed in. 'She almost passed out when she saw the blood. Luckily, I'd just got home from work but I wasn't taking any chances so insisted she come here.'

'Good thinking.' Jade had finished removing the bandage. 'Well, let's take a look.' Nicolette put the notes down, washed her hands and pulled on a pair of gloves as Jade manoeuvred a freestanding lamp into position. She elbowed a chair around the examination bed and sat down at the foot to examine the injury more closely.

'How is it?' Louise's tone was shaky. 'Has it stopped bleeding?'

'Yes. We'll just clean the area a little more so I can get a better look.' Jade handed Nicolette the things she needed. 'I'll need a magnifier headset,' she said softly to the nurse, before saying more clearly, 'I just want to be sure there are no other little bits around, otherwise we risk infection.' As she cleaned the wound, Louise flinched several times. Peering closely at it through the magnifier, Nicolette could see several particles of glass.

'OK.' She sat up and took off her gloves. 'There's still some glass in your foot so what we need to do is thoroughly flush out the area, which will hopefully remove the particles.'

'Will…will that hurt?' Tears formed in Louise's eyes.

Nicolette smiled reassuringly. 'I'm going to give you a local anaesthetic so you won't feel a thing.'

'Except the anaesthetic needle,' she whimpered.

'She's not good with needles either,' her husband ventured.

'That's all right. We'll get through it. Are you allergic to any medications?' Nicolette quickly checked Louise's notes.

'No. Not that I know of.'

Nicolette flicked back a few pages. 'It says here you had a local anaesthetic when you were fifteen.'

'My brother and I were arguing and we both fell down an embankment. We needed stitches.'

Nicolette nodded and showed Jade the notes so she knew what local anaesthetic to prepare. 'We'll give you the same anaesthetic you had back then as you didn't have a reaction to it.'

Jade quickly opened cupboard doors, getting things ready. 'OK. I want you to look at your husband, hold his hands and squeeze them as hard as you can.'

Jade held Louise's leg still, ensuring the woman didn't flinch as Nicolette administered the local.

'Louise? Louise?' her husband called.

'She's going,' Jade said calmly just as Nicolette was finishing. Sure enough, Louise had fainted. Jade attended to her, taking her vitals, calling to her.

'What's wrong?' her husband asked anxiously.

'She's fainted,' Jade replied, and a moment later Louise came around. Jade continued to monitor her. 'How are you feeling?'

'Is it over?'

'The injection part? Yes.' Nicolette smiled at her. 'It'll take about ten minutes for the area to be numb enough so I'll be back to check on you then. Jade will stay with you.' As she walked out, Sophie came up.

'Stephen needs you in Trauma Room 1. Emergency brought in by ambulance. Teenage boy complaining of arm, neck and shoulder pain.'

'OK.' Nicolette and Sophie went into TR-1 and headed to the sink. They both washed their hands before pulling on gloves and protective gowns.

'IV line, Sophie. Nicolette,' Stephen's voice was smooth. 'Meet Cecil.'

'Hi, there. Not been feeling too good?' Nicolette looked down into the scared face of the sixteen-year-old boy.

'My arms and shoulders are really sore,' he complained.

'Cecil's been burning the midnight oil for the past few days, studying hard.'

'I have mock exams.' No sooner were the words out of his mouth than he began to turn pale again.

'Does it hurt to look into the light, Cecil?'

'No.'

'Good.'

'Temperature is up,' a nurse reported.

'Abdomen?' Nicolette asked Stephen.

Stephen nodded and began to palpate Cecil's stomach. He pushed a little and received a groan from the patient. As he eased off on the pressure, Cecil groaned again.

'Does it hurt more *after* I finish pressing?' Stephen asked.

'Yes.'

Nicolette turned to look at Cecil's mother, who was standing at one side of the room. 'Has he had any pain-killers?'

'Two ibuprofen tablets but that's all.'

'Thank you. Urine analysis, full blood work,' Nicolette ordered.

'Are you allergic to any medications, Cecil?' Stephen asked.

'Not really. Sometimes I get stomach cramps from regular painkillers. I don't know what they're called.'

She looked down at the patient. 'Have you had bad stomach pain before?'

'A few times, but it's the cramps in my arms, neck and shoulders that are really sore.'

'A heat pack might give you some comfort.'

'Why do you care about his stomachaches?' Cecil's mother asked.

'Because that could be where the real problem lies,' Stephen responded. 'Sometimes when there's an infection around the abdomen, gases can form and they produce pain in the shoulders and neck.' He turned to look at Sophie. 'Contact the general surgical registrar and get him down here, stat.'

'Yes, Doctor.'

'BP's dropped slightly.'

'Get that fluid infused quickly. What's the result on the urine analysis?' Nicolette asked.

'Definite infection.'

'Right. IV ampicillin and morphine for the pain.' Stephen wrote up the notes. 'Nicolette, feel his abdomen,' he said softly.

'Appendicitis?'

'I don't think so. Something's not right.'

'Ulcer?'

'Can't be sure.'

Nicolette moved closer to Cecil. 'I'm sorry, Cecil,' she said as she touched his stomach. 'I just need to have a feel.' She did as Stephen had suggested but couldn't directly feel anything. 'Sorry,' she said after Cecil had groaned again.

'Temperature's going up.'

'Get that morphine into him.' No sooner had Nicolette spoken than Cecil started to retch. She managed to get a bowl to him in time and he vomited, the contents looking like coffee grounds with a trace of blood.

Stephen and Nicolette looked at each other. 'Tell the surgical registrar to book a theatre,' Stephen advised. 'Call the anaesthetists, too.'

'What's happening?' his mother asked in shock.

'I've got it,' Nicolette replied, and took off her gloves and gown. She took Cecil's mother into the waiting room and sat down beside her. 'Cecil has an infection somewhere and we believe it's in his stomach. As Dr Brooks mentioned before, the pain Cecil feels in his shoulders, arms and neck is more than likely due to a gas build-up inside.'

'But what causes that?'

'There could be several things but until the surgeons have had a look, we won't know for sure.'

'What will they do?'

'They'll do an exploratory laparoscopy, which is where they make a few tiny incisions—one just below the belly button and the other to the side. Next, they'll put a small camera into the area to see what's going on. What they find dictates what happens next.'

'But he just had some neck pain. That was it. That's why we came here. Not for this. Not to be told he needs morphine and then surgery.'

'I know it's not what you want to hear and I'm extremely glad you *did* bring him in. Cecil needs urgent medical attention and he's going to receive it. The surgical registrar will see him next but—'

'Why can't you or that other doctor operate?'

'We're not surgeons. I'll just check to see when we can expect the surgical registrar. Why don't you come and stay with Cecil?'

'Uh…all right. I guess so.'

They headed back to Cecil and Nicolette was pleased when the surgical registrar appeared a few minutes later.

'I need to check on a patient before her local anaesthetic wears off,' she told Stephen, before heading off.

'Louise,' she said as she breezed back into EC-2,

'how's the foot? Nice and numb?' Nicolette washed her hands again and pulled on a fresh pair of gloves.

'I think so.'

Jade helped Nicolette put the magnifier on and positioned the light. Nicolette tested that Louise's foot was indeed numb before debriding the wound. A few more particles came out but there was still one stubborn piece that refused to. Nicolette tried several times to grab it with the tweezers but it wouldn't budge.

'Locking forceps, please, Jade.'

Jade opened a drawer, pulled out what Nicolette needed and handed it over. Again, the piece of glass proved to be too slippery and after debriding one more time and making a very small incision to give her a bit more room to manoeuvre, Nicolette finally managed to remove it, breathing a sigh of relief as she did so.

'Hooray. It's all out,' she told Louise. 'I'm just going to check again to make sure there are no other sneaky pieces there and then we'll stitch you up.'

'Stitches?' Louise went pale again.

'Here she goes again,' he husband muttered, but his wife hit his arm, proving she was feeling better than he'd anticipated. Nicolette smiled but continued with her work.

Once she'd finished, she wrapped Louise's foot in a bandage and filled in a requisition form for crutches.

'Thank you so much, Nicolette.' Louise's husband pumped Nicolette's hand. 'You've been great.'

'Next time—' Nicolette said, smiling at Louise, but her patient held up her hand.

'I know, I know, don't walk around in bare feet.'

They all smiled and Nicolette left to write up the notes.

Later, near the end of their shift, she bumped into Stephen at the nurses' station.

'How's Cecil?' she asked.

'I've just had Sophie ring through to Theatre and it's not good. After the initial incision for the laparoscope, gas escaped.'

'As you suspected.'

'So they're doing a full check exploratory to see what they can find.'

Nicolette shook her head. 'What's your bet?'

'Ulcer.'

'Optimistic.'

'That's me. You think it's cancer?'

'I sincerely hope for Cecil's sake it isn't.'

'You and me both.' He shut the casenotes he'd just completed. 'Are you all done?'

'Yes. I was just going to get my jacket and think about heading home.'

'I was thinking that, too.'

She smiled at him. 'Great minds think alike.' He didn't return the smile but nodded. When he didn't say anything else, she forced herself to move away, heading to the changing rooms to get her things.

Nicolette pulled on her jacket, knowing it would be freezing outside…and foggy. She wondered how Stephen was going to cope, driving in the fog, especially after his earlier comments about not wanting Stephanie to drive home last night. The road between Katoomba and Blackheath was well lit but visibility could be down to a few feet and if you didn't know the curves in the road, it could be treacherous.

She decided to wait for Stephen and when he appeared in the main corridor, jacket on, briefcase in hand, she called out to him.

'I thought you might appreciate a guide on the drive back to Blackheath.'

'Thank you. That's very thoughtful.'

He came to stand before her and she saw he'd removed his tie and undone his top shirt button. Raking a hand through his hair, ruffling it slightly, she had an instant sense of *déjà vu* as a photograph of him flashed into her mind. Photograph. She watched him and concentrated hard before realisation hit.

'Simone.' She whispered the name and saw his eyes narrow slightly.

'Pardon?'

'Simone.' Nicolette nodded. 'I knew I'd seen you before. You used to date Simone.'

The colour drained from his face in a guilty admission.

CHAPTER TWO

'YOU'RE a friend of hers?' Stephen asked after a moment, his voice sounding slightly strangled, even though he did his best to hide it.

'Yes.'

'A friend who's interested in the truth or just what Simone told you?'

Nicolette couldn't believe him. Men! They were all the same. His comments, his facial expressions and the tone of his voice brought back memories of the way her own previous boyfriends had spoken to her near the end of the relationships. Just like Stephen, they'd always tried to dodge the blame. 'She almost had a nervous breakdown when you broke up with her, Stephen.'

His grip tightened on his briefcase as he made an effort to hold onto his temper. From the tone of her voice, he could see it would be pointless to discuss anything now. It was late, they'd both had a busy night and the last thing they needed was to argue before driving home on the foggy roads.

'Thank you for your offer to guide me through to Blackheath but I'll be fine,' he said politely. 'Drive safely.' With that, he walked out into the cold July night. A numbness encompassed him and he realised it had nothing to do with the mist surrounding him. As he unlocked his car and slid behind the wheel, Stephen wondered when his past was going to stop catching up with him.

One of the reasons he'd moved to the Blue Mountains had been to get away from the memories of the last few years, but it appeared they were determined to haunt him no matter what lengths he went to.

The fog was more dense tonight than it had been last night, if that was possible. He turned on his headlights and pulled carefully out onto the road, glad it was after midnight. There would be hardly any traffic to contend with except the trucks and they were usually lit up like Christmas trees.

Nicolette had been right when she'd said he didn't know the bends in the road but, travelling cautiously, he was able to slowly but surely navigate his way home to Blackheath, the fog becoming more dense around the area he now called home.

He garaged his car and headed inside, remembering to switch his cellphone back on. The instant he did, it rang. He checked the display—it was Steph. 'Hi.' He placed his briefcase on the benchtop and hung his keys by the door.

'Where are you?'

There was panic and strain in her voice and he wondered whether Nicolette had called his sister to tell her about his past.

'At home.'

'Oh.' She sighed. 'Thank goodness.'

'What's the problem?'

'You are. I started feeling depressed.'

Stephen closed his eyes. He and Stephanie had never been able to hide anything from each other, a bond which had formed in the womb. They *felt* each other and knew instinctively when the other needed help.

'I called the hospital but you'd already left. I was going to return the favour and have you sleep at my house. You know, it's probably not a bad idea for you to have a room here. That way, if the weather is bad when you leave the hospital, you can walk to my house.'

'I'll think about it.'

'Stephen,' she warned. 'I'm through stressing myself out worrying over you. First you had to deal with Mum's illness, then Simone stalking you and then last year…' Her voice broke on an emotional sob.

'Steph. I'm fine,' he reassured her. 'I'm here now and we're together again.'

'It's been too long,' she sniffed. 'You have no idea how your year in a war zone affected me. You're my brother. My *twin*. I *feel* you, Stephen. I know you've only told me half of what happened, but I felt your anguish, your desperation and your pain.'

He closed his eyes and raked a hand through his hair. 'Why do you think I didn't renew for another six-month stint? I knew it wasn't fair to you.'

She laughed but he could hear the sorrow in it. 'We make a hopeless pair.'

'Hope*ful*,' he corrected.

'So.' She took a breath and put on a bright voice. 'How was your first shift at the hospital?'

'Quiet.'

'Compared to what you've been used to, I can imagine.'

'That's right. No gunfire or bombs being dropped in the background or—'

'Stephen,' she warned.

He chuckled. 'Sorry. It was…unremarkable for a Thursday night.' As he said the words, his thoughts returned to Nicolette.

As though Stephanie picked up on that, she asked, 'And how was working with Nic?'

'Fine.'

'Just fine? You know, you never did tell me what you think of her.'

'She's an exceptional doctor.'

'So you're going to take her on in your practice? I knew it. I knew she was perfect.'

'I don't think so, Steph,' he said into the middle of her glee.

'What?' She stopped short. 'What do you mean, you don't think so? You just said she's an exceptional doctor.'

'She's a friend of Simone's.'

'Simone? Psycho Simone?'

'She wasn't psycho, Steph, just…clingy and with no self-esteem.'

'She stalked you, Stephen.'

'It was never proved,' he replied. 'Anyway, it won't work—Nicolette and I working together, I mean.' Any attraction he may have felt for the blonde doctor had to be suppressed. 'It was obvious tonight by her attitude towards me that she believed every word Simone had said about me, and she's entitled to. Simone was her friend and it's to Nicolette's credit that she believes her friend.'

'But there are two sides to every story. I'm sure once Nic hears yours, it will put everything right.'

'Leave it, Steph. I'm tired and it's late.'

'All right, but only because I love you.' She sighed with resignation. 'We should get your room here organised soon. As we are now firmly entrenched in winter, the fog settles in every night.'

'OK. You sleep well, sis. 'Night.' Stephen hung up and went over to the old gas heater which had come with the house. He switched it on, not impressed with the noise it made, but as it hadn't blown up last night, he thought he'd chance it once more. Tomorrow he'd do something more permanent about heating, like getting a slow combustion fire installed. He was really feeling the cold, especially coming here from a part of the northern hemisphere where the sun had well and truly been shining.

As he went through to the back of the house where his bedroom was situated, Stephen unbuttoned his shirt, his mind flicking back to the way Nicolette had looked him over at the end of their shift. She'd looked as though she'd wanted to devour him…until she'd remembered where she'd seen him before. He frowned. He couldn't recall being introduced to her, although at that time of his life there had been so much going on it was possible he'd forgotten. Usually, he had a very good memory.

Nicolette Bourgeois.

She was beautiful, no doubt about it. She was intelligent, too, and he hoped she was also fair and just. Usually it didn't bother him if people didn't like him. After all, you couldn't expect to get along with everyone you met, but for some reason Nicolette's low opinion of him mattered far more than he liked to admit.

Nicolette sat in front of the heater, determined to warm up and forget all about Stephen Brooks.

It was Friday and she was having a lazy morning as she didn't need to be at the clinic until midday and nothing was going to spoil it for her. She'd had trouble getting to sleep when she'd finally arrived home from the hospital, visions of Stephen refusing to leave her mind.

It had astounded her to finally remember where she'd seen him, and a lot of the things Simone had said about Stephen had come flooding back with a vengeance. He was untrustworthy, a manipulator and incapable of caring for anything or anyone…outside himself and his patients. He was cold, unemotional and totally self-centred.

Nicolette frowned. Funny, she couldn't ever remember Simone saying that Stephen had a sister. She'd met

Stephanie in January, but for the past six months every time the bubbly doctor had spoken of her brother there'd been concern, worry and pure love in her voice. Surely that showed Stephen was capable of caring for people not associated with his work. Even the short glimpse she'd had of the siblings together yesterday had shown how extremely close they were.

Nicolette had purposely driven past Stephen's home last night, just to make sure he'd found his way back home. As she'd rounded every bend on the drive between Katoomba and Blackheath, she'd half expected to find his car had skidded off the road, which would have served her right for not insisting he follow her back. Despite her feelings towards him, it was no reason to put his life in danger.

The light which she'd seen radiating from his new home—next door to the practice he was renovating—had instantly calmed her fears and she'd breathed a sigh of relief. He was home safe.

'You weren't going to think about him,' she muttered out loud, and busied herself by sorting through her nail-polish collection. Deciding on a colour, she prepared her toes and began painting. She'd almost finished one foot when her phone rang, startling her.

'Nic, it's Steph.'

'Problem at the hospital?'

'No. No. Sorry to disturb you on your morning off but I wanted to talk—'

'Good. I could use a good chin-wag.'

'About Stephen,' Stephanie finished.

Nicolette closed her eyes. Well, she'd been able to banish him to the back of her thoughts for a whole two minutes. 'What about him?' She worked hard to keep her voice neutral.

'He said Simone was a friend of yours.'

'News travels fast.'

'Stephen and I are twins,' Stephanie said. 'We...*feel* each other. It's hard to explain. Anyway, I just wanted to say there are two sides to every story. Stephen's a good guy and the past few years haven't been easy for him.'

Interesting. 'What happened?' The words were out her mouth before she could stop them. It was none of her business.

'It's not my story to tell, but what I can say is that he's a good, hard-working and trustworthy man.'

'You're a little biased, don't you think?'

Stephanie laughed but Nicolette could still hear the concern in her voice. 'Definitely. I never met Simone and I don't know all the details, but I do know she gave Stephen a hard time. Our mother was really ill at that point as well and...he... But anyway, when she died he took it personally. That's when he left.' Stephanie faltered, which was very unlike her, and Nicolette realised there was a lot more to what had happened than she'd been led to believe. 'Look, all I'm saying is give him a chance. I don't know whether you still keep in contact with Simone or not, but if you do, please, don't tell her where he is.'

There was fear in Stephanie's voice, which puzzled Nicolette. Before she could say anything to reassure her friend that she would keep quiet about Stephen's whereabouts, Stephanie groaned. 'I'd better go. Someone's just knocked at my door...probably wanting the roster changed. I can't wait to hand them over when the new director arrives. I'm never doing them again.'

Nicolette smiled. 'Hang in there.'

'You, too.'

When she put the phone down, Nicolette thought back to the last time she'd seen Simone. The other woman had taken her to Heathrow, making her feel guilty for returning to Australia when her time at the London hospital had been up. Actually, Nicolette had felt a little suffocated by Simone but hadn't said anything as there would soon be half a world between them.

The two women had become friends just after Stephen had broken off with Simone and the nurse had transferred to the hospital where Nicolette had been working in the A and E department. As they'd both just come out of relationships, they'd joined forces in slanging men in general and enjoying wallowing in their self misery.

'But I pulled out of it a lot earlier than Simone,' Nicolette murmured. For her final few weeks in London, every time she'd gone out with Simone she'd come home depressed after listening to the blonde nurse whine on about Stephen.

No. Even if Simone contacted her, she wouldn't say a word about Stephen. Nicolette also realised her behaviour to Stephen yesterday had been unfair but, still, the fact he'd already broken one woman's heart was evidence he could do it again. Nicolette had suffered enough emotional heartbreak with men to last her for quite some time. She herself needed to find a common ground with Stephen, especially if, as she hoped, they were going to work together.

'Colleagues—or if absolutely necessary professional acquaintances.' She resumed painting her nails, feeling better about the whole situation. 'Friends?' She asked the question out loud and immediately shook her head. Becoming friends with Stephen Brooks would make matters worse in the long run. She was already attracted to him and friendship would just muddy the waters, and she didn't need anything stirred up.

*   *   *

On Saturday night, Stephen turned up at the hospital ready for his shift. He punched in the code for the male changing rooms, stowed his briefcase in the locker and hung up his jacket, curious to see if Nicolette would be here this evening. Perhaps she'd asked Stephanie to change the roster so the two of them wouldn't be working together.

He took a deep breath and slowly exhaled as he hooked his stethoscope around his neck. It didn't matter whether she was here or not. Nicolette was nothing to him but a colleague—a fact he'd told himself ever since he'd walked away from her at the end of their shift the other night.

Stephen went in search of whoever was in charge that night and was surprised to find his sister there. 'Hey, kiddo.'

'Hey yourself.'

'You look flustered.'

'I am.' She thrust two files into his hands. 'EC-2 and EC-7 are for you. Nicolette's running late so you and I'll have to pick up the slack until she gets here.'

'Everything all right?'

'Car trouble.' Stephanie opened a new file and began writing as she spoke.

At least that answered one question, Stephen thought, a little surprised at the stirring of pleasure in his gut at the thought of seeing Nicolette again this evening…although he wasn't sure why. He glanced at the casenotes before heading into EC-2.

'Good evening, Mrs Bevan. Good evening, Sister.' He nodded to Sophie, who had just finished taking Mrs Bevan's blood pressure. 'I'm Dr Brooks.' He addressed his patient. 'I understand you're having some chest pain.'

'Ooh, it's awful, Doctor. Just awful.'

Stephen nodded and unhooked his stethoscope from his neck. 'Let's have a listen.'

'Any pain in your arms? Neck?'

'Both, Doctor, and I'm so worried about my Clayton. He's outside all on his own and it's going to be blowing a gale tonight. I hope he's all right.'

'Clayton?'

'My cat, Doctor. He's my baby.' She twisted a handkerchief in her hands.

Stephen nodded as Mrs Bevan continued.

'My neighbour brought me in here and then left to go and find poor Clayton to make sure he was all right. I was calling him, you see, getting him to come inside for his dinner and he wouldn't come. He usually comes immediately when I call him but not tonight, Doctor. Then I got worried and upset. Oh, dear.' She sniffed, tears welling in her eyes once more.

'I'm sure it's fine, Mrs Bevan. I'll have one of the nurses call your neighbour to check on Clayton's situation.'

'Oh, would you, Doctor? I'd be ever so grateful.' She dabbed at her eyes with her handkerchief. 'Thanks awfully.'

'Not a problem.' While Stephen had been talking to her, Sophie had been taking Mrs Bevan's vitals and she handed the chart to him. He read it quickly and nodded before writing up his own report, requesting a new set of scans and nitroglycerine should Mrs Bevan require it.

'I think we'll get you across to Radiology for a set of scans, Mrs Bevan, so we can get a better idea of what's happening.'

'But I've already had some scans,' Mrs Bevan rasped, looking quite pale.

'Tonight?'

'No. A few weeks ago. Dr River sent me here for some scans but when I saw him the other week for the results he said everything looked fine.'

Stephen glanced around for an X-ray packet but couldn't see one. 'Sophie?'

'I'll chase them up.'

'Thank you. I'll pop back and see you once your scans are done.' He smiled at the elderly woman.

'Oh, thank you, Doctor, and let me know about my Clayton.'

'Will do, Mrs Bevan.' Stephen headed over to the nurses' station and searched Mrs Bevan's notes for a contact number. There was no one around he could palm the call off on so he pulled out a chair and lifted the receiver. The dial tone was internal. He pressed zero and received the extended dial tone before dialling the required number. A moment later someone picked up the phone at the other end.

'This is Dr Brooks from the hospital. Is this Mrs Bevan's neighbour?'

'Yes. You don't sound like Dr Brooks.' The woman's voice was suspicious. 'In fact, you sound decidedly male. Is this a joke? Are you playing a prank?'

'No. No. I *am* Dr Brooks. Dr *Stephanie* Brooks is my sister.'

'Oh.' The woman's tone changed and she sighed with relief. 'I'm sorry.'

'That's fine.' Stephen explained the reason for his call and when he was assured that Clayton had indeed been found and was now safe inside the neighbour's house, eating his dinner by the heater, Stephen smiled. 'Thank you. I'm glad the cat's safe.' He rang off and made a note of the information.

He turned to find Nicolette standing behind him, a look of surprise on her face. 'Lost your cat?'

Stephen's eyes twinkled but he didn't smile. 'No. I don't own a pet. Merely checking up for a patient.'

'Oh.'

'Something wrong?' He stood, towering over her, and it was then she realised how close they were in the confined quarters.

'Er…no. I'm just surprised, that's all.'

'That I care about my patients?'

'That you care about their cats.'

'If it affects their mental and emotional healing, I care.'

'Holistic medicine?'

'Is there a law against it?' He stepped around the chair he'd just vacated and pushed it under the desk, the action bringing him even closer to Nicolette. She took a breath to say something then stopped as his spicy, clean scent floated around her. He smelt good…*very* good—and what she'd been about to say disappeared from her mind.

'*C'est bien,*' she muttered, unable to look away as their gazes held. Her heart was hammering wildly, so forcefully she was positive he could hear it without the aid of his stethoscope. Her lips parted as her breathing increased, allowing the pent-up air to escape softly rather than whooshing out of her in a rush.

'Listen, Nicolette.' His words were soft and the deep timbre of his voice vibrated through her, causing a swirl of tingles to explode within her. 'About the other night—'

'You're here, Nic.' At Stephanie's call, the bubble surrounding them burst and both shifted away, Nicolette bumping clumsily into the cupboard behind her.

Stephen reached out a hand to steady her but she smiled and waved it away. 'I'm fine.' She laughed with nervous tension as his sister came over to them. Stephanie looked from one to the other and when Stephen saw that knowing glint in her eyes he immediately knew he had to disappear.

'Right. I'll be in EC-7 if anyone needs me.'

'Don't forget about the cat,' Nicolette found herself saying, surprised her voice actually sounded fairly normal after the intense moment they'd just shared.

'Cat?' Stephanie looked from one to the other.

'Yes, the cat. Thank you.' He pivoted on his heel and went to see Mrs Bevan first.

'What was that all about?' Stephanie asked, looking at her friend.

'What was what all about?'

'You and Stephen.'

Nicolette forced herself to shrug nonchalantly. 'We were just talking.'

'Looked more like a staring competition to me. Sorry. Next time I'll make myself scarce so you two can connect without interruption.'

'What do you mean, *next time*? We were just talking,' she reiterated. 'We're colleagues so I think it might just happen again, Stephanie, whether you're around or not. You should be glad your staff are actually communicating.' She laughed, hoping her attempts to cover up the moment was working.

'Whatever you say.' Stephanie obviously didn't believe a word but let it drop.

'What have you got for me? And sorry again I was late. I think I need a new car.'

'Did you take a taxi here?'

'Yes.'

'Put in a claim form and the hospital can reimburse you.'

'It's fine.'

'It's protocol,' Stephanie pointed out. 'Believe me, I've become very familiar with protocols I never knew existed until I took on this job. Use them.'

Nicolette laughed. 'If you say so.'

'Patient in EC-9 is waiting for attention. Oh, and by the way, I'm counting on your sponsorship for my radical new hairdo.' Stephanie patted her red curls.

'You're really going through with it?'

'Sure am. Raising money for childhood cancer is a worthy cause. You know, you could always join me and get your gorgeous blonde locks cropped off.'

Nicolette instantly raised a hand to her hair, which was secured back from her face in a ponytail. 'I'm not as brave as you but you can definitely count on my donation. When is it?'

'Next Tuesday. Sarah from Oncology and Pierce from the MRI unit are also doing it, so you may want to sponsor them, too.'

'Sure.' Nicolette hugged the file to her chest and decided to get into the act of seeing patients before Stephanie emptied her bank account. She glanced at her patient's notes and headed into EC-9.

'Mr Stenton. I'm Dr Bourgeois.' Nicolette smiled politely at her patient and his wife, who was sitting beside him. 'It says in your file you've been having some abdominal pain.' Nicolette read the chart at the end of the bed as a nurse entered the cubicle.

'It's not good. I've had it for some time but tonight it got worse. So much so my wife had to drive me in and, let me tell you, that made the pain levels go through the roof.' He said the last bit in a conspiratorial whisper and then chuckled. A moment later he gripped his side in pain.

'See, Dr Bourgeois. That's what I mean. It's hard and it's sudden.'

'OK. Let's have a feel.' Nicolette washed her hands and pulled on a pair of gloves before pulling back the blanket and palpating her patient's stomach. Mr Stenton was a thin, wiry man and although she couldn't feel anything out of the ordinary, he groaned in pain when she touched him on the right side.

She checked his notes again. 'Medical history says you've had your appendix out.'

'Just after we got married,' Mrs Stenton supplied. 'Not a nice way to spend your honeymoon but very memorable.'

'So it was quite some time ago, then.'

'Oh, no.' She giggled. 'We've only been married for two years. It's the second marriage for both of us. Our children have all grown and now we have six grandchildren between us and another one on the way.'

'I'll bet you're looking forward to it.' Nicolette smiled at Mrs Stenton before writing up her findings. 'Mr Stenton, I'd like to run some tests—blood test, urine analysis—and also do an ultrasound.' She filled in the necessary forms and handed them to the nurse. 'I see you haven't been given anything for the pain. Are you allergic to anything?'

'No. Not that I know of.'

'Good.' Nicolette ordered a dose of paracetamol and codeine and signed off on the notes. 'I'll be back to check on you later.' She headed back to the nurses' station where Stephanie was frantically scribbling down notes, her ear glued to the phone receiver.

'OK. See you in five.' She replaced the receiver and looked up. 'Nic. Are you free? We have a gunshot wound patient and a police officer who's been stabbed, both ETA five minutes. You and Stephen have had experience with those so I'll need you both in TR-1.'

'What's the background?'

'A domestic. Neighbours called the police and by the time the police arrived the husband was threatening his wife with a knife. Police tried to talk him down but the man threw the knife at the cop and got him in the right side of the chest. Another police officer shot at the man to try and stop him, and the bullet has gone into his pelvis.'

Nicolette mentally went through the scenario in her head. 'What about the wife?'

'She was unharmed. The police are questioning her and then bringing her in to be checked out.'

'I'll get Stephen.'

'I'll call the necessary specialists we'll need and see if these people have patient files here.'

'Where is Stephen?'

'EC-7.'

'Thanks.' Nicolette headed over and walked into the cubicle. Stephen was sitting in the chair beside the bed, winding a bandage around his patient's hand. 'Dr Brooks. Can I have a word?'

'Certainly.' He finished what he was doing and stood, pulling off his gloves and pushing back the chair. 'That should do you fine,' he told his patient. 'Either go and see Dr Bourgeois here…' he indicated Nicolette '…at her clinic at the end of next week or come into A and E and we'll see if those stitches are ready to be removed.'

'Right you are, Doctor.'

'And remember to wear gloves next time,' he chastised good-naturedly.

'I've learnt my lesson, Doctor,' the man replied. 'Much obliged.'

Stephen took the notes with him and headed out. 'What's up?'

'Emergency coming in. Two patients. Gunshot wound to the pelvis and the other is stab wound to the shoulder. Stephanie wants us on the gunshot wound.'

He nodded. 'Let's go.' They headed into Trauma Room 1 where Sophie was getting things ready. They both scrubbed their hands and were assisted with gowns and gloves, ready for their patient. The paramedics wheeled the knife-wielding husband into TR-1, along with a police escort. The police officer who'd been stabbed was in TR-2 with Stephanie.

'Twenty-nine-year-old male,' the paramedic said as he gave the hand-over. 'Dale Hennesey. Gunshot wound to the right lower quadrant of abdomen. Penthrane given for pain relief, oxygen eight litres per minute. No allergies known. Patient alert and orientated.'

'Dale. I'm Nicolette. Do you know where you are?' she asked as they got into position to move him off the ambulance stretcher.

'In the hospital.'

'Good,' Stephen replied. 'Three, two, one, lift.' They transferred him across and the paramedics took their equipment and headed out. 'I'm Stephen Brooks. We'll get you sorted out.' Nicolette was inserting an IV into Dale's left forearm to get things started while Sophie was doing his observations. Another nurse was removing Dale's clothes, using a pair of heavy-duty scissors to cut through the fabric. The police officer stood to the side, watching what they did.

'BP 140 over 60, pulse 72, resps 22,' Sophie announced, and the scribe nurse wrote everything down on the whiteboard for all staff to see. Next, Sophie set up oxygen via a non-rebreather mask.

'How are you doing, Dale?' Stephen asked as he removed the padded bandage the paramedics had put on. 'Allergic to anything? Had a tetanus shot recently?'

'Not that I know of, and no,' he mumbled. It was hard to talk when wearing a cervical collar.

'Good. Maxolon 10 milligrams, morphine 10 milligrams, tetanus shot and Cephazolin 1 gram. Cross-type and match blood,' he ordered as he tossed the bandage aside and took a good look at the wound before him. 'Nicolette, I want you to check for an exit wound. The paramedics didn't note one but on the count of three, if we could just shift him a little to check.'

The staff followed Stephen's instructions. 'No exit wound,' Nicolette reported.

'Then the bullet's still inside. Order X-rays of right hip, abdomen and chest. Make sure the general and orthopaedic surgeons have been called.' Stephen didn't like the look of the wound site, and when Nicolette was free he motioned for her to take a look.

'There's more blood than there should be,' she said quietly.

'That's what I thought. Have you had much experience with gunshot wounds?'

'Plenty.' He obviously didn't know she'd also worked in a war zone, where she'd treated at least one gunshot wound a day. Then again, she supposed there wasn't any reason why he should know. She hadn't yet given him her résumé as she hadn't officially applied for the job on offer in his new GP practice.

'So have I. There's no time to take him to Theatre.' He turned to Sophie. 'Midazolam 2.5 milligrams,' he requested. 'We'll debride and take a closer look.' They scrubbed and gowned, working together, each reading the other's mind and doing exactly what needed to be done.

'BP's dropping,' Sophie called.

'He's bleeding internally somewhere.' Stephen searched the wound frantically, looking for the source of the problem.

'There. In there,' Nicolette said quickly, and held the retractor out for him to take, which he did. 'Hold still.' She grabbed a set of locking forceps. 'I can see the bullet. Once I remove it, take a look at the arteries.' She concentrated, the skill of removing a bullet coming back to her in a flash. In the next instant the tinkling sound of metal against metal could be heard throughout the room as the bullet dropped into the dish.

'Take the retractor,' Stephen said. 'Suction.'

Nicolette did as he asked.

'BP's still dropping,' Sophie said. 'Find it quickly, people.'

'Where are you?' he mumbled. 'Suction.' Although there was urgency in his voice, he still kept his cool. 'There.' With a satisfied nod, he clamped off the offending artery. 'Get an anaesthetist in here and book a theatre. How's his BP, Sophie?'

'Improving.'

'Good. One unit of plasma.' Stephen and Nicolette continued to check the area. Once they were satisfied with their patient's condition, Dale was taken to Radiology for X-rays.

'Thanks,' Stephen said. 'I'm glad you were around.' He tossed his gown and gloves into the appropriate bins.

'I could say the same about you.'

'Did you do trauma medicine long?'

'Six months normal, six months highly intense. I much prefer GP work. I like to follow through with patients.'

'I know what you mean.'

'I've had too much…excitement in both my working life and private life. I want steady and easy and comfortable.'

Stephen frowned at her words, amazed at how her thoughts mirrored his own. He acknowledged her words with a slight inclination of his head. 'I need to check on Mrs Bevan.'

'The cat lady?'

'Yes. Once she knew her darling was safe, her heart rate settled into a more normal rhythm. She said she saw Dr River the other week. He sent her off for scans but apparently they came back clean.'

'So?'

'The woman has angina and isn't on any medication for it.'

'What are you implying?'

'I'm not implying anything. I'm merely stating facts. I would like to ask, though, what your opinion of Dr River is, but it will have to wait. How about coffee in the tearoom in twenty minutes? Does that suit you?'

'Emergencies notwithstanding, yes.' Nicolette tried not to smile like a Cheshire cat. It was only coffee *and* in the tearoom where they'd be easily reached if an emergency came in. It was nothing special. At least that's what she told herself as she went off to check on Mr Stenton and Stephen headed off to see his cat lady.

Mr Stenton had just returned from his sonogram with the report. Nicolette read it with interest.

'Gallstones,' she told her patient and his wife.

'But you haven't got all the test results back in yet,' Mrs Stenton protested.

'Did the sonographer show you the scans she took?'

'Yes. We could see the stones quite clearly,' Mr Stenton said, patting his wife's hand reassuringly.

'I'll hand you over to the general surgical registrar and he'll take over your care from here.'

'Will he need an operation?' Mrs Stenton asked, her voice trembling.

'I'm not sure. Sometimes the stones can be broken down through a technique called lithotripsy, where sound waves are administered via ultrasound—similar to the one you've just had. Most times the stones then pass normally through the system, but the registrar will be able to tell you more.'

'Thank you, Dr Bourgeois.'

'You're more than welcome.' Nicolette headed back to the nurses' station, wrote up her findings on Mr Stenton and left a note for the general surgical registrar. When she checked her watch, she realised it was way past twenty minutes since she'd seen Stephen. She went to the tearoom, wondering if he was still there. He was.

'You only just made it,' he stated as he stood and made her a cup of coffee. He asked about milk and sugar and she gave her order. He stirred the sugar in slowly, watching her all the time before handing it over—not saying a word.

Once he was seated again he took a sip from his cup and swallowed. She watched the action of his Adam's apple, amazed at how gracefully he did everything. Nothing was ever hurried or forced. Even when he'd been treating Dale Hennesey he hadn't allowed himself to be rushed.

'Tell me about Dr River.'

Those were the words which eventually came out of his mouth and Nicolette almost groaned. He'd been looking at her, his blue eyes full of meaning, and that had been the last thing she'd expected him to say.

Nicolette thought carefully, also pleased it was her turn to make him wait. 'He's ready to retire,' she said eventually, and Stephen nodded as though he'd been expecting her to say those exact words all along.

'Do you think he's becoming a little…lax in his treatment of patients?'

Nicolette chose her words carefully. 'He has been leaving a lot of the day-to-day consulting up to me.'

'Tactful.' He nodded as though he approved. 'I like that.'

'How's Mrs Bevan?'

'Doing just fine. I've admitted her overnight for observation but she'll be at home and reunited with her cat tomorrow morning. I've also put her on angina medication, which should help control her symptoms a lot better.'

Nicolette smiled. 'I'm glad she's going to be reunited with her cat. She's such a sweet lady.'

'We need to discuss the new clinic,' he stated matter-of-factly.

'We do?'

'I thought you wanted to work in my clinic.' What he'd seen tonight had impressed him and it also seemed that, whatever Simone had said about him, it didn't matter to Nicolette—at least as far as her professional life went. He respected her for that.

'You want to work with me?'

'You seem surprised.'

'I just thought…' She trailed off and looked at him, searching for something in his face that might indicate he was joking. 'I haven't even given you my résumé.'

'I've seen quite a bit the past two shifts we've worked

together.' He stood and carried his empty cup to the sink. 'Are you free tomorrow?'

Nicolette spluttered on the mouthful of coffee she'd sucked in. Quickly recovering, she coughed a few times before looking up at him in puzzlement. 'Tomorrow is Sunday.'

'Correct. Are you free?'

'Er…yes.'

'I'll pick you up at ten. Does that suit?'

'Pick me up? You mean as in a *date*?' she asked incredulously.

CHAPTER THREE

NICOLETTE saw humour light up in Stephen's eyes and a slight tug at the corners of his mouth. 'You can call it a date if you like, but don't get upset if we start discussing business.'

She was still taking in his words as he walked from the room and realised he'd been teasing her. She groaned and slumped forward, putting her head between her knees. A *date*? Why on earth had she said that out loud?

And the effect his ever so slight smile had had on her? Devastating. Seeing the brightness of amusement catch in his blue eyes was rocking her senses and she was glad she'd been sitting down. The man was enigmatic and she was captivated by him, eager to know more, wanting to find out just what made him tick.

It was a bad sign. She'd vowed not to get involved with another man...at least, not for some time. Although Simone had told her plenty of stories about the handsome Stephen Brooks, Nicolette knew she had to trust her own instincts, especially if she was going to work with him. She needed to put aside all Simone had said and form her own opinions. The problem was, she couldn't deny the attraction that existed between them.

'*Attention.*' She warned herself as she stood and took her cup to the sink. It was good advice because if she wasn't careful, she'd end up making an enormous fool of herself and that was the last thing she needed.

Nicolette headed back out to the nurses' station where she found Stephen talking to Lauren, the pretty brunette.

The nurse was smiling up at him as she spoke and although he didn't share her smile, he was listening intently. Nicolette felt an instant dislike for Lauren zap through her and she quickly pushed it away. Stephen was nothing more than a colleague so why did Lauren's attempts at flirting bother her so much?

The nurse laughed and Stephen smiled politely, his standoffish attitude making Nicolette feel a little better. It seemed to say, You can flirt all you like, lady, but it isn't going to get you anywhere. The problem was, he seemed to be like that with her as well, and *that* she didn't like.

Stephanie came up at that moment and slumped down into a chair. 'I'm wiped out.'

'How long have you been here?' Stephen put his hands on his sister's shoulders and began to massage them. Lauren, who'd been angling for his attention, fired mental daggers at Stephanie. Nicolette hid a smirk, realising the nurse had no idea the two doctors were related.

'Since eight this morning.'

'Go home.'

'Ooh, that feels good.' She leaned her head back and looked up at him. 'Don't forget to pay up big with your sponsorship.'

He groaned and dropped his hands. Nicolette couldn't help but laugh. 'She's conned you, too, eh?'

'When *doesn't* she con me? Ever since she could walk, she's been conning me.'

'Really?' Stephanie smiled. 'I thought it started in the womb. Mum always said I took up most of the room.'

'Which was why I had to get out at the first available opportunity,' he replied drolly. 'Hence, I'm the oldest.'

'And you haven't let me forget it since.'

'Oh, my gosh! You two are related?' Lauren had just caught up.

'We're twins,' Stephanie replied.

'Go home,' Stephen reiterated as he reached for a set of casenotes. 'Nicolette and I can hold the fort for the next few hours until our shift is over.'

'Sure?'

'Of course,' Nicolette assured her. Stephen's answer was simply to glare at his sister.

'All right. I'm going.' She kissed him on the cheek. 'Don't have too much fun without me.' She winked at Nicolette, which gave a whole new meaning to her words.

Nicolette turned away, feeling herself begin to blush, and concentrated hard on making sure the pens on the desk were neat and tidy. Stephen picked up a set of casenotes and headed off to an examination cubicle. She glanced up, watching him walk, his back straight, his shoulders square, his long legs striding with purpose. He had a nice walk…and a cute butt. Lauren sighed and it was then Nicolette realised they'd both just been standing there, watching him.

'What a dish, eh?' she murmured as she picked up a file and handed it to Nicolette. 'I wonder if he has a girl-friend.' She snorted. 'Probably. All the good-looking ones are taken.'

Nicolette headed off to her new patient with that thought in mind. Did Stephen have a girlfriend? If he did, where was he hiding her? And also why would he be asking her out if he did? She stopped her thoughts. *She* had been the one who had called it a date, but still it probably wouldn't hurt to find out if he was currently attached. Not that it would mean anything to her. He was just a colleague.

The next few hours flew by and she hardly saw him until they were both coming out of the changing rooms at the end of their shift. Stephen stopped when he saw her

and waited, then they continued down the corridor together, their briefcases between them like a barricade.

'Stephanie mentioned you had car trouble.'

Nicolette groaned. 'Don't remind me.'

'How did you get here?'

'Taxi.'

'How are you planning to get home?'

'Taxi. I was just going to ring for one.' She stopped by
a house phone as if to prove her point.

'I'll take you.'

'No. It's all right. It won't take long for the taxi to
come. Besides, Stephanie said I'd be reimbursed for the
expense.' She was babbling so to stop herself she picked
up the receiver and started to dial.

Stephen took the phone out of her hand and replaced it
on the hook. 'I'm going to Blackheath and you don't live
far from me. Let me take you.'

A brief war waged inside her. What he said made sense
but she didn't want to put him out—although he'd just
said it wouldn't be an imposition, which meant she could
accept. Then again, she'd be in his car…close confines of
his car…with him so…close to her. Perhaps an imper-
sonal taxi was better in the long run—at least for her
pounding heart.

In the end Stephen made the decision for her by placing
his free hand gently beneath her elbow and propelling her
in the direction of the hospital front doors. Nicolette gave
up the war and followed his lead.

They walked out into the cold night and her first
thought was it might take them longer to get back to
Blackheath. Usually it was a fifteen-minute drive. Tonight
they'd be lucky to do it in thirty.

'I think it's worse than Thursday night,' he said as he

unlocked his car and they both quickly got in. 'If that's possible.'

'At least I'll be able to make myself useful by guiding you around the curves,' she said, and then realised how her words might be misconstrued. 'Of the road,' she added lamely, feeling herself beginning to blush. Thank goodness it was dark.

'Of course,' he said, but she could hear the amusement in his voice. He started the engine and pulled out of the car park.

'Do you ever smile?' she blurted out, and he briefly glanced her way. '*Really* smile, not just polite ones for the staff and patients.'

'Of course.' Again that amusement was still in his voice.

'Most people smile at least once a day.'

'Give me something to smile about and I'll smile,' he replied indulgently.

'At least Stephanie makes you smile.'

Stephen nodded. 'She always has.'

'You're very different. Chalk and cheese.'

'Isn't that usually the way with twins?'

'I wouldn't know. I'm not a twin. Stephanie's bubbly and vivacious and so out there.'

'While I'm not?'

Had she offended him? She hadn't meant to. 'I didn't mean it like that. Your sister is about to shave her head. I mean, to me that's out there.'

'To me, too.' He shrugged. 'Stephanie's just… Stephanie, and I love her dearly. The past few years haven't been easy for her.'

'That's what she said about you.' Nicolette thought for a moment. 'It must be hard, always having to think how your actions or reactions might affect her. I mean, if something were to happen to you, she would *feel* it, wouldn't she?'

Stephen took in her words. 'Yes.' He exhaled slowly. 'Sometimes it is hard, but the good far outweighs the bad.' He thought his words out carefully and Nicolette waited patiently. 'I've always had company. I've never been alone. Even in some of the darkest moments of my life, Stephanie's always been with me through this connection we have. I don't have to explain myself and there are no repercussions. She instinctively knows and understands me, and it's an amazing feeling.'

Stephen's words made Nicolette think of Simone and again she wondered what had really gone on in that relationship as what she'd seen of Stephen and what he'd said didn't gel with what Simone had related.

'It sounds great. My brothers haven't a remote hope in understanding me, although I'm not sure they've tried all that hard.' She laughed. 'Still, they love me and that's important.'

'That's very important. Are they older than you?'

'Yes, and they never let me forget it.'

'An older brother's prerogative.'

Nicolette laughed at his remark and thought she caught a glimpse of a smile on his lips. Nah—she must be dreaming. She stared out into the foggy night, wanting to deepen their discussion, but knew now wasn't the time. Instead, she gave him tips as to which lane he should be in to handle the curves more easily.

'At least at this time of night there's not much traffic to contend with,' she said into the silence that surrounded them. It was as though they were in their own little world, a world of whiteness, lit only by the headlights of Stephen's car. They crawled along, thankfully not running into trouble or seeing anyone else in trouble.

Nicolette gave him directions to her house after he'd turned off into the streets of Blackheath. 'Thanks, Stephen,' she said after he'd pulled into her driveway. She undid her seat belt and turned to face him. The front sensor lights had come on, illuminating the white mist around them. Even so, the extra light meant Nicolette could see him more clearly than before. He was squinting a little at the sudden light but had also shifted a little to look at her.

'My pleasure.' He said the words in his usual calm, controlled manner—just as she was coming to expect. 'I'll see you tomorrow at ten.'

Nicolette nodded slowly, knowing she should get out of the car but finding herself unable to move. 'Stephen, about Simone…'

'It's late, Nicolette.'

'I want to apologise for my behaviour. It was a bit of a shock when I finally realised where I'd seen you…or rather your face. Simone had a lot of photos of you.'

'Hmm.'

'Stephanie said it wasn't a good relationship for you.'

Stephen exhaled harshly and shook his head. 'Stephanie doesn't know when to keep her nose out of my business.'

Nicolette smiled. 'Isn't that what pesky little sisters do?'

'Yes.' He nodded. 'Thank you for apologising and I hope you'll accept mine in return.'

'Done. We'll start tomorrow with a clean slate. What do you say?'

He paused for a moment, as though totally amazed. 'Good idea.'

Then it happened.

The corners of his mouth twitched upwards into a slow smile. It wasn't a toothy grin, it wasn't merely a smirk. Her breath caught in her throat at the sight and she glanced momentarily at his blue eyes to find them looking intent yet relaxed.

'Wow,' she whispered, then cleared her throat. 'You should do that more often.' Her words were soft and in that one second the atmosphere in the car changed from one of camaraderie to one of intense awareness on both sides. 'You look really different when you have something to smile about.'

'Thank you for providing the reason.' His deep voice washed over her.

'What did I do?'

His smile increased a little more at her surprise. 'You showed your worthiness.'

She nodded slowly, her heart hammering wildly in her chest. 'So worthiness is rewarded with smiles. I'll have to remember that.'

'You do that.'

Both of them could feel the undercurrents of a completely different conversation happening while they sat there staring into each other's eyes.

After another few seconds she roused herself. 'I'd...uh...better go in.' Nicolette pointed to her house.

'OK.'

The smile was starting to fade and she had a desperate urge to do something—*anything*—to keep it in place. 'I'll see you tomorrow morning.' She picked up her bag from the floor and opened the door.

'Nicolette.'

The pounding of her heart increased as he said her name. Was he going to smile again? Was he going to lean across and kiss her? Her lips parted in nervous anticipation. 'Yes?'

'Dress warm and comfortable. We'll be doing some walking.'

'Oh. OK. Thanks.' She quickly climbed from the car and shut the door, feeling instantly foolish. How could she even think he'd kiss her? The man hardly knew her and even though they'd just shared an intense moment, it was no indication he was ready to press his lips to hers.

When his car didn't move, she realised he was waiting to make sure she was safely inside and the chivalrous act earned him extra brownie points. After she'd unlocked and pushed open her front door, she turned to wave and he slowly reversed. She leant against the closed door, listening to his car as it went slowly up her street. It wasn't far to his place but the fog was still extremely thick.

She stood at the door, waiting for her heart rate to return to normal. What had she been thinking? She'd been flirting with him—just like Lauren back at the hospital. Surely she was better than that?

Of course she was. She'd made him smile.

The knowledge instantly warmed her, even though her house was cold. Finally, she managed to get her legs to work and walked over to the heater, turning the setting to FULL. 'After all, you can't live off warm memories with Stephen Brooks for long,' she warned.

Even though she told herself to calm down, not to read anything into the moments they'd shared, she couldn't help the thrill of excitement at the thought of seeing him tomorrow. Dress warmly. She frowned, wondering where he'd planned on taking her—and at ten o'clock in the morning.

'You're starting to think seriously about this guy,' she growled at herself as she changed into a russet-red tracksuit. It was fleecy and warm, just like her ugh boots. She wandered through to the kitchen and switched on the kettle. 'You've been hurt too many times before,' she admonished herself five minutes later as she sipped her cup of tea. 'He'll break your heart,' she finally concluded as she rinsed her cup and headed for the bathroom.

Once she'd brushed her teeth and climbed into bed, she snuggled down beneath the covers, a small smile on her face and her head still full of thoughts of Stephen.

Maybe just for tonight she could dream about him. After all, one night couldn't hurt...could it?

Nicolette rushed around the house, looking for her gloves, stressed out because she couldn't find them and she'd just heard Stephen's car pull up outside. 'Why did he have to be so punctual?' she muttered as she continued searching. She knew she shouldn't have expected anything less from him. He definitely seemed the type of man to not only be punctual but also meticulous.

Was he meticulous in *everything* he did?

She blushed as she remembered parts of her dream, and in her dream Stephen had kissed her as no other man ever had or ever would. She shook her head, snapping herself out of fantasy land and back to reality as she started pulling underwear out of her drawer. The doorbell rang just as she'd finished emptying the contents onto her bed. Still no gloves.

She groaned with impatience and frustration as she rushed to the front door, not wanting to keep him waiting. She'd taken him at his word and dressed as he'd suggested, warm and comfortable. She was wearing a pair of denim jeans, two pairs of socks and her favourite walking boots, which she'd broken in two and a half years ago when she'd gone walking in Wales. That had been with Tim. Tim had come before Warren and Warren had come before Archie. Archie had been the last man she'd let break her heart and since then she'd forced herself to concentrate on other things besides relationships.

Now, here she was opening the door to Stephen Brooks and effectively putting herself out there once more. This time, though, she'd be smarter and keep her wits about her, and that meant no more dreaming about heart-melting smiles and heart-pounding kisses from the delicious doctor.

The instant she opened the door, she knew she'd have to strengthen her resolve.

He stood there in a pair of jeans—not covered in paint—and a thick jumper, with a bright, striped scarf around his neck. His nose was a little pink from the cold and puffs of steam were coming out of his mouth as he breathed. 'Good morning, Nicolette.' When she didn't say anything, he continued. 'If you're ready, we'll get going.'

'Uh…come in for a second. I can't find my gloves.'

He stepped quickly over the threshold and closed the door, not wanting to let the cold morning air into her warm house. She led him into the lounge room. 'I won't be long.'

Stephen stood on the spot and looked around the room, surprised to find it so…homey. There were bookshelves across one long wall and photographs on the others. Two large comfortable sofas were facing each other with a coffee table between. There was a cabinet which housed a television, DVD player and a stereo, as well as CDs and several DVDs.

At the other end was an open fireplace which was tidy and all set up with wood ready to light. The walls around the room looked as though they needed painting but for the most part it was a very comfortable room. Stephen wasn't sure what he'd expected but he was pleasantly surprised not to find the room decked out with modern furniture and the latest colour trends.

He wandered over and checked out her gas heating unit.

This was the type of thing he needed, and even though the slow combustion fire he'd had installed was working a treat, it didn't quite heat all the way to the bedrooms.

It was a few more minutes before Nicolette returned, her hands still bare.

'No luck?' he asked.

She shook her head, a frown creasing her brow. 'I don't know what I've done with them. I'm sorry to hold you up, Stephen. I'll get my coat and we can go.' Nicolette disappeared again and Stephen headed back out to the front door to wait. She returned a moment later, winding a brown scarf around her neck and pulling a matching woollen hat over her head, the blonde ends of her hair sticking out around her face and shoulders. She looked warm, cosy and…inviting.

Stephen cleared his throat and his thoughts. She was a colleague. Today was a test for her to see if they could work well together. Medically, he had no hesitation in offering her a job and if she passed the tests he had for her today, he'd have a clearer vision about his practice.

Nicolette stuck her hands into her coat pockets, thinking she'd have to leave them there all day if she was going to have any feeling left in her fingers, then she gasped in astonishment and pulled out her gloves.

Stephen's eyes were bright with repressed mirth. 'So that's where you put them.'

Nicolette pulled them on and then grabbed her handbag. 'Let's go.'

'You have a very nice home,' Stephen said as he reversed out of her drive.

'Thanks. My parents bought it when we were kids. We lived in Sydney and would come up for holidays or long weekends. Luc lived here for a while a few years back and now it's my turn.'

'And your parents?'

'They're travelling. They say they've earned the right to see the world. Last I heard they were in Seattle, visiting old friends.'

'Good for them.'

Nicolette took a breath, knowing what she was about to say could have drastic repercussions on the rest of the day but if they were going to be working together they needed some sort of background on each other. Besides, he was asking about her family. 'Stephanie told me your mother died a couple of years back.'

'Correct.' His mask slipped instantly into place.

'She said it was when you were dating Simone.'

'Correct.'

'That must have been hard for you.'

'Meaning?'

'I know how…demanding Simone can be. Did she know your mother was ill?'

'No.'

'Don't you think you should have clued her in? I mean, she was your girlfriend.'

Stephen gripped the steering wheel tighter, holding onto his temper. 'I thought we were going to start with a clean slate today.'

'Yes. Sorry. We were. I apologise.'

'Accepted.'

'It's just you were asking about my family so…' She left her sentence hanging. Stephen sucked in a deep breath and slowly exhaled, and she had the feeling he was desperately trying to hold onto his temper.

'You're right. My mother died of lupus and my father died when Steph and I were teenagers.'

'It's great, then, that you're living close to each other again.'

'Yes.' His tone had gentled in that one word and Nicolette breathed a sigh of relief. They were back to the beginning.

'What's on the agenda for today?'

'Different things.'

'Sounds interesting. I think.'

Her words were rewarded with one of Stephen's rare smiles. 'I'm glad you think so. I also appoint you as navigator. Stephanie told me I should go and see Mermaid Cave, and as you've been visiting the district for most of your life, that makes you the expert.'

'Gee, thanks. OK. In that case…' Nicolette glanced out her window '…I think you're going the wrong way. Did Stephanie give you a map or something?'

Stephen handed it over and Nicolette checked the map, turning it around in her hands so it faced the way they were going. 'Yes. You've come down too far. Go back and take the third right.'

Stephen glanced over to look at the map. 'You've got it upside down.'

'Don't go there,' she warned. 'I've had numerous…shall we call them *discussions* with my brothers over the different ways men and women read maps. You've appointed me navigator so just keep quiet and do as you're told. If not, *I'll* drive and *you* can navigate.' Nicolette knew that would be the worse option.

'You're right. I'll keep quiet. Third on the right it is.' He made the turn and they went down a steep hill.

After a few hairpin bends, Nicolette instructed him to pull into a small dirt parking area. 'We need to walk from here.'

'Have you been to Mermaid Cave before?'

'Many, *many* years ago.'

'But not since you've come to live here.'

'No.'

'Then it'll be an adventure for both of us.' Stephen climbed from the car and went to the boot where he took out a backpack. He'd packed a bottle of water for each of them, small energy snacks and a basic first-aid kit. He pulled on his coat and scarf before shrugging the backpack on. Next he pulled a camera from the boot and then closed it and locked the car. Puffs of steam came from their mouths, their noses pink due to the cold. 'Ready?'

'Yes.' Nicolette buttoned up her coat, tucked her scarf in and made sure her gloves were on properly. 'Nice camera,' she said, noticing the telephoto lense. 'Digital?'

'No. I confess that's one area I haven't wanted to explore yet. I find it strange not loading film into a camera before I use it.'

'Fair enough.'

'Besides, this gives me better quality for painting scenes.'

'You don't paint in person?' They headed off down the path.

'How else would I paint if not in person?' he teased.

'You know what I mean. You don't bring your easel out here and sit down and paint the scene?'

'Sometimes yes, sometimes no. If I find something today I want to paint, I'll take photographs first and then decide whether it's necessary to come and sit out in the freezing cold to capture what I want, or whether I can do it from the photograph.'

'Fair enough.'

They continued walking, stopping every now and then when Stephen found a view he liked. Sometimes he'd take a photograph of one very small flower, other times he'd go for a panoramic shot. Nicolette was relaxed and happy, remarking on the differences of their surroundings from her childhood memories.

When they rounded one bend they came across a sign saying the path was closed. 'What?' Nicolette read the sign again. '"No further entry due to unsafe surface."'

'Looks as though the winter weather has done some damage,' Stephen remarked. 'Pity.'

'Yes, it is. You would have liked the view from the cave.'

'They should have had a sign at the beginning of the track.' Stephen was puzzled.

'Maybe we missed it.'

'Anyway, let's head back.' They did as he suggested. 'I'll come back in summer and check it out then.'

Nicolette noticed he spoke in the singular, not the plural, and felt an immediate pang of loss. Why should he include her in his plans? she questioned inwardly. They were colleagues, that's all. Snap out of it, girl.

She pushed the thought away and followed him back the way they'd come. When they reached the car he put his camera away and took off the backpack. Nicolette looked around to see if there was a sign and eventually she found it.

'There it is.' She slid down a small embankment and retrieved the sign before climbing back up.

'What are you doing?'

'Just getting the sign.'

'You could have twisted your ankle or hurt your arm.'

'It's not that steep, Stephen.' The sign and the post had come apart. 'Looks like vandals or either a very, very strong wind.'

'My bet is vandals.' She pulled off her gloves and tucked them into her pocket again.

'Let's get the sign back together and put it up where it

can be seen.' Stephen grabbed his toolbox from the car boot and carried it over. He handed Nicolette a hammer and some nails and was impressed when she took them and nailed the sign back onto the post, which was still in the ground at the beginning of the track.

'Good job, Dr Bourgeois.'

'Why, thank you, Dr Brooks.' They returned to the car and as Stephen packed away his tools Nicolette took off her scarf, coat and hat. 'That's warmed me up.'

Stephen checked his watch. 'We're a little bit early for the next item on my agenda but if you don't mind eating now, we'll have a longer, more leisurely lunch.'

'At the Megalong Tearooms?' she asked, climbing inside the car and doing up her seat belt.

'How did you know?'

She smiled. 'It's the only place to eat along this road. We're in the Megalong Valley so the Megalong Tearooms is *the* place to go. Besides, they have the most amazing food there.'

'So I've heard. It's one of Steph's favourite places.'

'She's not the only one.' Nicolette smiled as they continued to drive through the valley. 'It's so beautiful here.' There were lush green hills with native Australian trees on one side and cliffs on the other—the town of Medlow Bath at the top of the cliff. 'Slow down and turn right into the next driveway,' she instructed.

As they climbed out, Stephen saw several picnic tables outside the building which was a house with the front section converted into a restaurant and serving area. 'Do you want to eat outside or inside?' Nicolette asked.

Stephen looked up at the sky. 'I think we'll chance it outside.'

'I was hoping you'd say that.'

She smiled brightly at him and he felt his stomach

clench. She'd left her woollen hat in the car, pulling on her coat and scarf, and as she turned to walk up the steps to the servery, she tossed her blonde locks behind her.

She was beautiful and there was no denying it. He liked her in her casual clothes of jeans and a thick jumper rather than the brisk business suits he'd seen her in up until now. She seemed more…approachable like this and he wasn't sure that was a good thing. How was he supposed to keep his distance, maintain a level of professionalism when he couldn't help but find her immensely attractive?

He followed her up the wooden steps.

'You *have* to try their homemade pies. They're the best.'

'What about you?'

'Oh, that's easy. Homemade soup. Perfect for this sunny winter's day. That way, I can leave room for dessert.'

'Dessert?' He raised his eyebrows.

'You can't come to the Megalong Tearooms and not sample one of their desserts! Perish the thought.' She laughed, her eyes bright and alive with happiness.

'You really love it here, don't you,' he stated.

'How did you guess? It's so close to where I live yet far enough removed from the world that a person can really relax and unwind, even if it's just for a few hours.' She gave the lady behind the counter her order and Stephen did the same. Then, to his surprise, she grabbed his hand and tugged him back down the steps and around to one of the picnic tables. She let go once they were at the table and sat herself down. Stephen could still feel an imprint of where she'd touched him and he shoved his hands into his coat pockets to compensate.

'So…' She searched for a topic, her gaze settling on his scarf. 'That's an interesting scarf. Nice and bright.'

'Stephanie made it.'

'I thought so. I can't see a stripey scarf of bright yellow, green, orange, red and blue being one you'd choose in a men's store.'

He smiled. 'No. Steph made it as a birthday present and sent it to me just before I left London.'

'Where did you go after London? I know you've been away for the past year, and when I met Stephanie earlier this year she was always so very worried about you.'

'I was working for a medical relief organisation in Africa.'

Nicolette processed the information, also taking in the warning tone of his voice. 'Not much call for a stripey scarf there.'

'No.' He relaxed. 'Still, it made me feel close to her.'

'You obviously did two six-month stints. Which organisation did you go with?'

Stephen hesitated. Why did she want to know? Was she making small talk or did she want to psychoanalyse him? Try and figure out why he'd gone? He named the organisation and she nodded.

'I did six months with them eighteen months ago.'

Stephen looked at her in complete amazement.

'Don't look so surprised. They let women doctors in, too, you know.'

'Yes. Of course.' He thought for a moment. 'That's why Steph wanted you and I treating the gunshot wound patient yesterday.'

'Makes sense now, doesn't it?'

'I had no idea.'

'You think you're the only one who can run away?'

'I wasn't running—'

Nicolette held up her hand. 'Bad choice of words.

Sorry. I was running away and I was wrong to imply you were doing the same.'

'Why did you run?'

'Bad relationships. Why else? It was after Warren and before Archie.'

'A bit drastic to put yourself in constant danger just because of a failed relationship.'

'A bit drastic to put yourself in constant danger just because your mother died,' she countered softly. She watched his jaw clench tightly and shrugged. 'I'm sure you ended up finding out more about yourself during your stint there, just like I did. Putting your life in constant danger can certainly help get things in perspective.'

'True.' He decided to ignore the comment about his mother. 'So what did you learn?'

She thought for a moment. 'Not to be so gullible, I guess.'

'Where men are concerned?'

'Mainly.'

'Yet you said you went there after Warren and—'

'And before Archie,' she finished. 'That's right. Warren broke my heart and I ran away. When I came back, I worked in London and that's when I met Archie.'

'And were you gullible?'

A slow smile played across Nicolette's lips. 'No. I saw right through him and broke it off. I haven't dated anyone since.'

'And you met Simone when?' he asked.

'I thought we weren't going to talk about her today.'

Stephen shrugged. 'Let's get her out of the way once and for all.'

'I met her about a week after I broke up with Archie.'

'Let me guess, you talked about how untrustworthy and commitment-phobic most men are.'

'Are we that predictable?'

'Women in general? Or just you and Simone?'

Nicolette was happy to see the teasing glint in his eyes. 'I don't know if I want you to answer.' She chuckled and surprisingly Stephen joined in.

'So you saw through Archie and haven't dated anyone since?'

'That's right. After my experience on the frontline, I felt...' She searched for the right word. 'Disconnected is probably the best way to describe it. Once I'd broken up with Archie, I realised I needed to find out who I really was before I even thought about getting into another relationship.'

Stephen nodded thoughtfully. Wasn't that exactly where he was? Feeling disconnected? Not wanting to get into a relationship? It was a timely reminder that he should change the subject to a more neutral topic.

'And while we're on the subject of Simone,' Nicolette continued, before he could speak, 'I wanted to say again how sorry I am for the way I treated you the other night.'

'You've already apologised.'

'I know, but I've had time to think about the things she said about you and even though I've only known you for a few days, I've realised none of what she said was true. You're a good man, Stephen.'

He nodded slowly then looked away, unable to believe how touched he was. 'Thank you.'

Nicolette sighed and then smiled at him. 'Whew. I'm glad I got that out in the open.'

Their food arrived and the conversation turned to more general matters as they devoured the delicious food. 'You were right. The fresh apple strudel was amazing.'

'I don't know. The warm banana loaf was delicious as

well.' Nicolette licked her lips as though to prove it. 'Mounds of fresh cream also helps. *Très bien.*'

'Agreed.' Stephen had been quite surprised when Nicolette had cut both desserts in half so they could share them. It had been quite…intimate yet he hadn't felt that screaming sense in his gut that she was moving too far too fast. Odd. Perhaps it had something to do with the bond they shared of working in a war zone. It was an experience hard to describe unless you'd actually lived it. He'd also been surprised by Nicolette's accurate perceptions of him, but once more he hadn't felt the need to run. This morning he'd been determined to test her, to see if they could find common ground which would enable them to work together as colleagues. Now, he realised, he'd got more than he'd bargained for.

He'd found someone who was on his wavelength.

CHAPTER FOUR

'So what's next?' Nicolette rubbed her hands together.

'Getting cold?'

'Not yet. We've been here for well over an hour and although I'm stuffed full of good food I'm ready for whatever else is on your agenda.'

'We'll use the conveniences, then head back to Blackheath.'

Nicolette chuckled as she stood.

'What?'

Her wide smile was once again in place and it instantly warmed Stephen's heart. 'It's just been a long time since someone told me to go to the toilet before I get into the car.' She headed off before he could say anything and soon they were back in the car, driving through the tranquil scenery once more.

'It's so beautiful here,' she murmured into the comfortable silence they'd shared since leaving the tearooms.

'That it is.'

'You know, one time when we were out on a retrieval mission after some heavy fighting, we were captured and driven to an enemy camp in the middle of nowhere. I was forced to operate on the group's commander. Let me tell you, it's not easy operating when there's a gun trained on you.'

'I know.'

Nicolette smiled without humour. 'Yes. I'll bet you do. Anyway, once the operation was complete they wanted to take us to another camp to operate on another soldier.

71

Thankfully we were rescued by our people on the way.'
She shook her head. 'Naturally, I was relieved to be rescued but I'll never forget…as we came up over a hill, the
sun was just starting to set and there before me was the
most breathtaking view. In a country full of deceit and
corruption with the smell of death in the air, there was
beauty. I realised right then that I needed to take more
time to appreciate the everyday miracles. The trees, the
birds, the sky, the clouds, the sun.' She paused. 'This is
one of those places that just gives me everything in one
hit.' Nicolette sighed. 'Given that you were in similar circumstances to me…' she reached out and covered his
hand with hers '…I'm glad to be sharing this moment
with you. It seems…right somehow.'

And it did. Her touch wasn't sexual or have any im-
plication other than shared experiences, and he appreciated it. She held his hand as they drove along the valley
floor, both absorbed once more in the scenery. She removed it when they started the steep, winding climb up
the hill to Blackheath.

'I love living here.'

'It's very…picturesque,' Stephen agreed. He continued
driving through the main street of Blackheath and then
down to a landscaping centre.

'What's happening now?'

'Firewood.'

'Pardon?'

Stephen drove into the landscaping centre and parked
the car. 'I need firewood,' he repeated, and climbed out
of the car. He came out of the centre a little later and
moved the car, reversing it into place so he could attach
a trailer. Once that was done, he drove over to the wood
pile. Nicolette kept looking around her, trying to figure

out what was going on. Usually, if she needed firewood, she had it delivered.

'Coming?' he asked as he climbed out of the car once more.

She followed him and saw him pull on a pair of gardening gloves and start selecting pieces of firewood from the pile and putting them into a trailer. Nicolette raised her eyebrows in disbelief. 'You want me to put that wood in that trailer?'

'Yes.'

'But there could be spiders and all sorts of things in that wood pile.'

'Spiders are what you're concerned about? This from the woman who operated with a gun pointed at her?' He shook his head, bemused. 'The spiders—if there are any—will be down at the bottom. Choose bits from up the top.'

'But I might break a nail. That really hurts, you know.'

He nodded, reached into the back seat of the car and pulled something out, tossing it at her. She caught it, only to discover it was another set of gardening gloves. 'That'll help.'

Nicolette glared at him for another minute, mumbling in French beneath her breath. She'd been having such a good time until now. Why did he have to go and spoil it by being all…male?

Stephen chuckled as her mumbling continued and she glared at him, desperately trying not to let his smile crack through her peevishness.

'So is this where you bring all your dates?' she eventually asked.

'Who said this was a date?'

'You di—' She stopped, remembering what he'd said yesterday. *You can call it a date but don't get upset if we start discussing business.* Nicolette nodded as she pulled on the gloves. 'I get it. This is a test. You're testing me. You've probably been testing me all day.'

Stephen's only answer was a smug 'I'm in control' smile. She glared at him, wanting nothing more than to wipe it off his face. Even so, she couldn't help the way he was affecting her equilibrium. She stumbled forward, concentrating on him rather than where she was putting her feet, and he quickly reached out a hand.

'You all right?'

'I'm fine. Right. Test away.' She picked up a piece of wood and put it into the trailer. One after the other, they loaded the trailer. Soon she was climbing up onto the pile to pick better pieces and Stephen was amazed at how quickly she adapted.

'You know,' she said once the trailer was almost full, 'I need firewood, too, although I'd planned on getting it delivered. Instead, you can just deliver half of this to my house.'

'That'll mean I'll have to come back sooner to replenish my stock.'

'Then that can be our second…date,' she retorted, heaving another piece of timber onto the pile. They covered the trailer, tying it off with Army knots before admiring each other's handiwork.

'Not bad.' Stephen nodded.

'Yours are a bit shabby,' she teased.

'They are not. They're perfect. Just check out that tension.' It was only when he looked at her that he realised she was teasing. 'Very amusing,' he replied drolly. Stephen had the trailer weighed, then he paid and drove them directly to Nicolette's house where they unloaded half the wood.

'No. Not that piece,' she said, tossing it back. 'That's yours. *That* piece is mine.'

'Typical female,' he mumbled as he took the piece she'd pointed to. Once her wood was stored in the shed next to the house, Stephen knew it was time to say goodbye. He'd had an amazing day, better than he'd hoped, but it was starting to move towards late afternoon and he had the feeling if he didn't say goodbye soon, they'd end up sharing dinner together. That hadn't been part of his initial plan, despite how tempting it was.

Before he could say a word, though, she'd climbed back into the passenger seat and shut the door.

'What are you doing?' he asked as he climbed behind the wheel. 'You can go inside to keep warm.'

'I'm actually *very* warm after all that manual labour.'

'Then why are you in the car?'

She frowned, confused. 'Aren't we going to your house to unload your wood?'

'I was going to take care of that myself.'

'Oh, no. No, no, no. You can't just say you're testing me and then cut me off halfway through the test. If I hadn't snagged half this wood for myself, you'd have had me at your house unloading the entire trailer, so let's go, Brooks. Time is awasting.'

She had a point so Stephen shut the door and drove the short distance to his home, reversing the trailer into the drive. When they'd finished unloading it, they returned the trailer and this time Stephen was determined to take her home and say goodbye.

'Come in for a drink,' she urged as he walked her to the door.

'I'm fine.'

'I know you're thirsty after all that huffing and puffing you were doing. Besides, I think it's only fair if you tell me if I passed the tests.'

'You did. With flying colours.'

'I take it that means I get the job?'

'Yes. I'll have a contract drawn up for you.'

'Thanks, but we have more to talk about than that. Don't you want to know about Dr River and his practice? The patients? What the main demographic is? What type of salary I expect?' She grinned at the last one.

Stephen hesitated for a fraction of a second longer than necessary and Nicolette took that as a positive sign. 'Cold or hot drink?'

'Both, if you don't mind,' he said as he followed her into the house.

'Water? Tea?'

'Great.'

Nicolette turned the heater on and headed into the kitchen. Stephen wasn't sure whether to follow or head to the homey lounge room he'd been in that morning. She made the decision for him.

'Browse through the bookshelves, look at the photographs. There are some cute ones of me, even if I do say so myself,' she called with a laugh.

He did as he was told and had a close look at the photographs. He'd become more intrigued by Nicolette as the day had worn on and the opportunity to have a sneak peek at her childhood was something he wasn't going to pass up.

There was one photograph of her at the famous Three Sisters rocks in Katoomba. She was flanked by two boys. She looked about seven years old in the photograph. Next to it was another photograph, taken probably ten years later, in the same place with the same people in the same poses. It was interesting to see how much all three children had changed, but where Nicolette had been wearing pigtails and a toothless grin in the first one, she was definitely a maturing teenager in the second. Both brothers were well over six feet and had protective arms around their sister. Being protective of his own sister, Stephen knew exactly how they felt and he was glad Nicolette had someone looking out for her.

She came back with two glasses of water and placed them on the coffee table. Stephen stayed where he was, looking at the photos. 'How old are your brothers?'

Nicolette glanced at the photos and smiled. 'Luc's thirty-six and Pierre's thirty-five. I'm thirty-three, just in case you were wondering.' She stood beside him and looked at the photo, smiling with the memories it evoked.

'How did they react when you went to a war zone?'

'Luc had already been so he understood. Pierre was a different kettle of fish. He learned to live with it.' She pointed to another photograph, one taken in a professional studio. 'That's the last time we were all together. Three years ago.'

'Before Warren?' He couldn't resist asking.

'Before Tim even. Tim was before Warren.'

'Miss them?'

'My ex-boyfriends?' she teased.

Stephen's answer was to glare at her.

'Oh, my brothers. Yes. Terribly.'

'What do they do?'

'They're both doctors,' she said with a smile. 'I know. Luc says we all copied him, but we're all in different specialities.'

'And where are they?'

'Pierre's in Perth and Luc's in Launceston.'

'Do you catch up often?'

'We call each other weekly. Both of them came to pick me up from the airport when I returned home from London and we had a week together in Sydney before I came here.'

'It's good to be with family.' He said the words more to himself than to her.

'You missed Steph?'

Stephen frowned a little in concentration. 'I don't *miss* her as such because she's always with me but, yes, I missed her. We can have conversations where no words are needed but we know exactly what the other is thinking.'

Nicolette nodded slowly, her heart racing as she shifted closer to him. 'So…if I were to, say, kiss you right now, Stephanie would know?'

Stephen was taken aback at her forthrightness. 'Uh… I…er.' He stopped and cleared his throat, surprised at how warm the room had suddenly become. 'She wouldn't *know* exactly but she'd, er…feel an emotion.'

'How are you supposed to keep anything secret from her, then?'

Stephen was mesmerised by this woman. She shifted closer still and although he felt like backing away, he stood his ground. She was dangerous and up until that moment he hadn't realise just *how* dangerous she could be to him. Then again, he'd flirted with danger before and was still alive. He was sure he could do it again and still remain unhurt.

Her brown eyes were now deep and intoxicating, drawing him in. Her lips were slightly parted, ready and waiting to receive his. He was totally captivated and at that moment he could think of nothing he wanted more than to have the mutual need they were experiencing satisfied.

'With great difficulty.' His mind was at odds with his words as he answered her question, his gaze flicking from her mouth to her eyes and back again.

'I love a challenge,' she whispered, bringing her body up against his. She gasped at the immediate awareness of him. He may not have physically moved since she'd come back into the room yet the mental distance they'd covered was huge. Although she still had strong reservations, it felt right. Besides, she was a grown woman. She'd learned a lot about herself in the past year and she was positive she could keep control of the situation and not let her heart get muddled up in things. At least, she *hoped* she could do that.

She glanced up at his mouth, her tongue unconsciously slipping between her parted lips to wet them in sweet anticipation. He groaned. The sound was deep and low in his throat, giving it a primeval, animalistic sound, one that washed over her with a wave of electric excitement. Her want…her need grew in that one moment and her desperation to have his mouth on hers intensified.

Their hands, hanging by their sides, brushed lightly together. The mere contact caused heart rates to soar, their fingers to entwine. With an almost imperceptible tug he urged her even closer, his other hand coming up to rest at her back.

Her heart was pounding so wildly against her ribs she was positive he could hear it, and at that moment she didn't care. The thought that her emotions were now at the point of no return was irrelevant and something she pushed aside, not wanting to even think about the implications of her actions. The way he made her feel was the only thing that mattered.

Stephen felt a churning in his gut. It was so powerful, so intense his eyes widened at the sensation. His fingers clenched around hers, gripping tight as he took his other hand away from her back and slammed it up against the wall for support. Then nausea hit him like a tidal wave and he groaned, unable to move.

It took a few milliseconds for Nicolette to snap out of

her fantasy world and realise something was wrong. 'Stephen?' She glanced down at their hands, clenched tightly together. He was groaning again but this time it was with sheer agony. 'What's wrong?'

He coughed. 'I don't know.'

He was really sick, she realised, and clicked into doctor mode. She freed her hand from his, pressed one hand to his forehead and the other to his carotid pulse. 'Stephen! You're burning up.' He coughed again and closed his eyes. Nicolette urged him to sit on the floor before he fell down, and the fact that he went willingly indicated he wasn't well. 'What happened? Why are you so sick all of a sudden?' She reached for one of the glasses of water she'd brought in and raised it to his lips. He sipped gratefully before coughing again.

'Get my phone,' he rasped. 'It's on my waistband.' Nicolette did as he asked.

'I'll be right back.' She quickly found a hand towel, which she wetted through then squeezed out. She was back by his side before he could open his phone. She took the phone from him and placed the cold compress to his forehead. 'Who do you want to call?'

'Steph. I need to check Steph.'

Nicolette's eyes widened in astonishment. 'You think something's wrong with Steph? Are you...*feeling* her?'

'Call her.' He coughed again. Nicolette scanned through the names in his cellphone until she came to Steph's. She dialled the number and waited. And waited...and waited.

'I'll try the hospital.' She called through to switchboard but was told Stephanie wasn't in the hospital. Nicolette got them to page her and waited, but still no Stephanie. 'Call me if she comes in or if you hear from her,' Nicolette said.

'No!' Stephen whispered, feeling helpless. 'Have some-one go around to her house. Have them check it out.' Nicolette relayed the information to the switchboard op-erator before hanging up. 'We need to go to her house.'

'Stephen, I don't want you moved. They'll find her—'

'No.' He shifted up onto his elbows. 'She's not all right. This is *her* I'm feeling. This isn't me. I'm not sick. *She* is.'

Nicolette wasn't so sure but decided to follow his lead. After all, he was the one who'd lived with these feelings all his life. 'OK. Let's get you up, then. Well have to take your car not only because it's parked in the driveway behind mine but because mine's dead anyway,' she mum-bled, remembering she still needed to do something about it. With her help Stephen rose to his feet but the instant he was vertical he immediately felt nauseous again. 'Take it easy,' she soothed. She handed him some water and he rinsed his mouth. 'Feel better?'

'Yes. Keep going.'

They slowly made it out to the car, Nicolette stopping to grab only their coats and her house keys. He rinsed his mouth once more and then actually straightened to his full height, a bit of colour starting to infuse his cheeks once more.

Stephen managed to open the driver's door but Nicolette steered him around to the passenger side. 'You're in no shape to drive, buddy. Come on, give me your keys.'

'I'm not drunk, Nicolette.' His tone was brisk and haughty and she couldn't help but chuckle.

'You sounded mighty British then, old bean. Give me your keys, get in and keep quiet.'

He reluctantly fished his keys from his pocket and did as he was told. She went around to the driver's side and climbed behind the wheel, adjusting the seat position and the mirrors. Stephen merely muttered something about having to put it all back later but she just smiled again as she put her house keys into the glovebox.

'Ooh, drives nice and smooth,' she purred as she reversed onto the road. 'Thank goodness the fog hasn't come early tonight.' She headed to the main street and turned left onto the road that led to Katoomba. By the time they passed through Medlow Bath, a few minutes down the road, Stephen was able to sit upright, no longer groaning or coughing, and even in the dim light she noticed more colour and strength returning with each passing kilometre.

'Feeling better? You're certainly looking it.'

'Much. Thank you.' His phone rang and he quickly answered it. 'Dr Brooks.'

'Dr Brooks? I was looking for Dr Bourgeois,' the hospital switchboard operator said.

'She's driving. Have you found my sister?'

'Yes. It was freaky. We sent someone around to check like Dr Bourgeois told us to and there was smoke coming out of her house. The neighbour's house was the same. The fire department's been called but the person I sent couldn't find Stephanie,' she clarified.

'We'll be there in ten.' He disconnected the call. 'Stephanie's house has smoke coming from the windows.'

'It's on fire!' Nicolette was alarmed.

'Sounds that way.'

'No wonder you were coughing.' She thought for a moment, then nodded. 'Fever, nausea, coughing. It all adds up.'

'Just drive,' he snapped.

'You *are* feeling better, aren't you? Back to your old bossy self.'

'I'm sorry. I'm just worried.'

'Understandable.' She noticed he was becoming calmer the closer they got to Stephanie's house. It was a strange sensation to actually see the link operate between the twins. She was close to her brothers but nothing like this and in a small way she envied their closeness.

They remained silent, Nicolette concentrating on driving and Stephen concentrating on his sister, his eyes closed, his forehead creased in deep thought. Her heart went out to him and she knew in that instant that he was a man of value, of principle and ethics.

She drove past the hospital and up the hill towards Stephanie's house. They could hear the sound of fire engine sirens behind them and a moment later Nicolette glimpsed the flashing lights in her rear-view mirror just as she turned into Stephanie's street.

Even before she'd brought the car to a complete stop, Stephen had undone his seat belt and opened the car door. 'Stephen!' Nicolette tried to call him back but he disappeared into the smoke which was now filling the area.

She cut the engine and was out of the car just as fast, running after him. She grabbed his arm and hauled him back.

'You can't go in there.' She pointed to Stephanie's house.

'I'm not. She's in there.' He pointed to the neighbour's house.

'Stephen. It's on fire!'

'Thank you.' He wrenched his arm free and took two more steps before she grabbed him again. He rounded on her with repressed fury. 'You don't understand.' His teeth were clenched, his face full of certainty. 'I know where she is. I have a clear picture in my head. I can save her.'

'Stephen?' Nicolette had no idea what to do.

'I couldn't save my mother but I can save my sister,' he said, and wrenched himself free of her once more, heading into the thick smoke. She could do nothing except watch him go. The smoke was becoming worse and Nicolette coughed, heading back to the street, wringing her hands together anxiously. She'd been in worse situations—and so, she reminded herself, had Stephen. He'd be OK.

She said those words over and over in her mind as she spoke to the firefighters, letting them know there were at least three people in the neighbour's house.

Nicolette watched with increasing apprehension as the firefighters went about their job. She checked her watch. Two minutes. Three minutes. Five minutes.

Where was he? He'd said he'd known exactly where Stephanie was! Why hadn't he got her out by now?

The smoke was thick and black and she forced herself to switch off from the worry and actually do something productive. She checked the boot of Stephen's car and found a first-aid kit as well as the water bottles he'd packed for their walk earlier that day. She opened the medical kit and checked it closely, glad it was fully stocked. An ambulance siren briefly pierced the air, the sound getting louder until it abruptly stopped as the vehicle turned into the street, its blue and red flashing lights illuminating them.

The police weren't far behind and the narrow street Stephanie lived in was now blocked with vehicles.

Nicolette glanced at her watch again. 'Come on, Stephen.' Eight minutes.

'Over here,' she heard someone call, and watched as a figure came through the smoke, carrying a woman in his arms.

'Stephen!' She grabbed the bottle of water and first-aid

kit and rushed over, relief swamping her. He carried his sister until they were well away from danger then he knelt down and placed her on the ground. Nicolette looked up and called to the paramedics. 'Oxygen, stat.' She turned back to him. 'What took you so long?' she demanded. 'I thought you knew where she was!'

Stephen collapsed back onto the grass, coughing and spluttering. 'I'm glad to see you, too,' he choked out. She felt Stephanie's pulse. 'Where's that oxygen?' she called, and a paramedic appeared by her side. 'Get a mask onto him as well.' She indicated Stephen. 'Steph? Stephanie? Can you hear me? It's Nic. Steph?' She checked her breathing, listening closely, and was glad to find her friend breathing. 'Steph?' she called again, and this time received a cough as a reply.

'Nic?'

'Yes, it's me.'

'Stephen?' Her voice was weak and raspy.

'He's here. He's fine.' At least, she hoped he was. Nicolette gave her a sip of water then glanced across to find him swatting away the oxygen mask the paramedic was trying to put on him. 'Yes. He's fine. Stubborn but fine.' Her words made Stephanie smile a little.

'That's my bro.'

Nicolette reached for the mask beside Stephanie. 'I want you to have some oxygen. Breathe deeply now. That's it,' she said once she'd fitted the mask and Stephanie had started breathing.

'Mrs Malincotty?'

'Your neighbour?' Nicolette asked as she draped her friend with a blanket. 'I don't know. The firefighters are taking care of things.'

'But she was—'

'Just relax, Stephanie. Doctor's orders.' Nicolette checked

her for burns, cuts and bruising but thankfully found nothing. 'I'm just going to check on Stephen.' She shifted around to face twin number one. 'Put the mask on, Stephen.' She reached for it and went to put it on him.

'I'm fine.'

'Oh, no, you're not. You're in so much trouble you're going to need all the oxygen you can get just to fight with me, mister.'

'Fight? Why are we going to fight?'

Nicolette leaned closer so her words didn't carry. She didn't want to upset Stephanie. 'I can't believe you just went into the burning house. If you'd waited another minute, the firefighters would have been able to get her out.'

'She's my sister.' He coughed.

'See what I mean about needing the oxygen? Now, do as you're told or I'll be winning all the bouts.'

'Hmm.' He reached out and placed a hand around her neck, drawing her closer. Before she knew what was happening, he'd pressed his lips to hers and she found herself floating in a place of utter peace, the chaos around them momentarily wiped from her memory. She closed her eyes and concentrated on him, on what the two of them felt like together.

His mouth was surprisingly soft and she felt herself turning to jelly as she knelt beside him. Even though the cool evening air had started to swirl and mix with the smoke, she was warmed through by the sensations he was evoking. It was everything she'd dreamt about the night before…and more.

She opened her mouth a little, loving the taste of him. It was as though they were caught in a bubble of time, time which was passing with a delicious slowness, allowing them to experience each and every emotion. Pleasure, surprise, eagerness, passion. Those and many more ripped through her as she felt his lips open beneath hers, the tip of his tongue teasing her even further.

She gasped and drew back slightly, looking down at him, unable to believe what had just taken place. It was brief but meaningful, the intensity taking both of them by surprise.

'Wh—?' She stopped and cleared her throat. 'What was that for?' she managed to whisper.

'You just won round one. I was enjoying the making-up part.' He took the mask from her and placed it over his mouth and nose. 'Bring on round two.'

CHAPTER FIVE

THERE was a shout from one of the firefighters and Nicolette reluctantly tore her gaze from Stephen.

'Doc. Over here.'

She rose to her feet and was astonished when Stephen tried to sit up. 'Stay there,' she ordered.

'I'm OK.'

'Stephen! Just do as you're told for once.' She motioned to one of the paramedics. 'Make sure he stays here and keeps the mask on.' Without a backward glance she headed over to where the firefighters were carrying out an elderly woman. Someone quickly placed a blanket on the grass before the men put the woman down.

'She's not in good shape, Doc.'

'Oxygen, stat.'

'Here.' Stephen knelt down beside the woman. 'Grab a new mask,' he ordered the paramedic. 'She can use this unit.'

'Mrs Malincotty,' Nicolette called, and received no answer, her fingers automatically checking the woman's pulse.

'She's not breathing,' Stephen reported at the same time Nicolette discovered the woman's pulse was very weak. He grabbed the medical kit the paramedic had placed beside them and reached for a face shield and gloves. Within seconds he was ready and had Mrs Malincotty's head tipped back, ready to perform expired air resuscitation.

Nicolette began to count as he performed the breaths, getting ready to perform chest compressions. Together they worked for what seemed like an eternity, Nicolette's voice calmly counting so they kept perfect time. While they did their job, she noted the burns to the patient's lower arms and hands.

'I need wet towels. Patient has burns to her arms and hands.'

'I'm on it,' someone called.

After a minute, Mrs Malincotty choked and spluttered, coughing. Stephen turned her head to the side and Nicolette checked her pulse.

'It's stronger. Mrs Malincotty, I'm Nicolette. I'm a doctor and a friend of Stephanie's. This is her brother, Stephen. I'm just going to put an oxygen mask on you to help you breathe more easily.' The person with the wet towels returned and Nicolette carefully wrapped her patient's frail hands in them while Stephen spoke to the patient, letting her know he was going to check for other injuries.

'Can you remember what happened?' Stephen asked, but all he received was a mumbled confusion of incoherent words. The only one he understood was *Stephanie*.

'Stephanie? Stephanie's doing just fine,' Stephen assured her. 'My little sister's a tough cookie. Don't you worry about her.' He continued checking for fractures while Nicolette intubated the patient. 'Right hip feels displaced.'

'Acknowledged.'

He checked Mrs Malincotty for medic-alert ID but couldn't find any.

Nicolette reached into the first-aid kit but couldn't find what she was looking for. She turned to the paramedic who was assisting them. 'Can you get me some midazolam and also get ready for patient transfer?'

The paramedic returned with what she needed and

Nicolette drew up the injection. 'Mrs Malincotty, I'm going to give you something which will help with the pain while we move you.' Her patient began mumbling again. 'It's all right. We're going to take you to the hospital.'

The midazolam worked quickly and with the aid of the paramedic and two of the neighbours who had come out to help, they were able to lift the blanket beneath Mrs Malincotty onto the ambulance stretcher.

'Go with her,' Stephen instructed. 'I'll get Steph to the hospital so she can be checked out.'

'I'd prefer you not to drive.' Nicolette said. 'Go in the ambulance. There's enough room.'

'How will you get there?'

'I'll drive your car. I'd rather keep a close eye on both you and Stephanie.'

'Really, Dr Bourgeois? Don't you think that's a bit possessive of you?' He paused and leaned closer, his breath fanning her cheek as he teased softly. 'And after only one kiss.'

Nicolette's eyes widened in disbelief and for a moment she thought she'd imagined his words. She literally shook her head to make sure she wasn't going crazy. 'Pardon?'

He merely shrugged but didn't move away. 'You heard.'

His close proximity was blocking the logical signals her brain was trying to send out. All she could think about for that moment was him…and her, their lips reunited in a passionate kiss.

A loud noise around her pulled her out of fantasy land and back to reality. Nicolette cleared her throat. What had he said? That she was possessive? She hoped he really didn't think so because that wasn't what she'd meant by her comments. Nicolette felt the need to defend herself, to tell him she wasn't being possessive but a good doctor who cared for her patients. She opened her mouth to speak but he turned his back on her and headed over to his sister, effectively ignoring her.

First he'd refused to put his mask on, then he'd rocked her world senseless with that kiss, then he'd defied her instructions to stay put and now he'd not only teased her but disappeared before she could think of a suitable retort.

The thing was, she was pleased to find him in such good humour after what had just transpired. It appeared the dashing Dr Stephen Brooks didn't count rushing into a burning house to rescue his sister as anything too traumatic. Besides, she kind of liked him when he was in teasing mode.

He soon returned, with his sister by his side. One arm was around Stephanie's waist, supporting her, and in the other hand he carried the oxygen cylinder. At least his sister was following orders, the oxygen mask still on her face.

'Let's go, Dr Bourgeois.' They didn't stop as they passed Nicolette.

The paramedic who'd been monitoring Stephanie volunteered to pack up and also stay and keep an eye on the firefighters in case any of them became sick. Nicolette thanked him and headed to the ambulance. Stephen was settling his sister in the front seat of the ambulance while Nicolette climbed into the back to check Mrs Malincotty was comfortable for the short trip. Stephen came around to close the door as the other paramedic climbed into the driver's side.

'I'll follow in my car,' he stated.

'I'd rather you didn't drive.'

'I'll see you soon,' was all he said and shut the doors in her face. Nicolette seethed impatiently inside. He was a law unto himself and although he might be the most wonderful kisser on the planet, he was a pain in the rear when it came to following orders.

The ambulance set off and within a few minutes they were at Katoomba hospital. Nicolette went with Mrs Malincotty, leaving Stephen and Stephanie to look after each other. She gave a hand-over to staff on duty, answering their questions and filling out the paperwork. By the time she'd finished, not only was she exhausted physically but mentally as well.

Stephen found her in the tearoom. 'Just as I'd suspected.' His deep voice washed over her and she opened her eyes. 'Sitting down on the job, feet up, eyes closed, enjoying a drink. Think you're off duty, Dr Bourgeois?'

'Yes. As a matter of fact, I do, Dr Brooks. How's Stephanie?'

'Fine. How about Mrs Malincotty?'

'She's being seen by the burns specialist regarding her hands but respiratory-wise she's stable. They'll be moving her to ICU tonight and, depending on the extent of her burns, they may transfer her to Sydney tomorrow. Is Stephanie staying in for observation?'

'Ha! My sister? No. She's refused to stay overnight so I'm taking her home with me.'

'Good thinking. That way I can keep an eye on both of you.'

'Pardon?' He came and sat down beside her.

'I'll stay at your place, too, so I can keep an eye on both of you.'

'I don't need you to stay. I can take care of Steph myself.'

'I'm sure you can but who's going to take care of you?'

'I am.'

'Uh-huh, and what if you have a delayed reaction to the smoke you inhaled? When you came out of that burn-

ing house you refused to lie still, you refused to keep the
oxygen mask on. I'm sorry, but I'm only trying to protect
my investment.'

'Investment?'

'You've asked me to come and work with you and if
my boss keels over due to respiratory problems, that
would leave a lot of extra work for me.'

'Nicolette, I don't need—'

She stood and glared down at him. 'Tough. I'm looking
after both of you troublesome twins tonight, and that's all
there is to it.' She took her cup to the sink and rinsed it
then turned back to face him. He opened his mouth to
speak but she held up a hand. 'Forget it, Brooks. You can
call me possessive or concerned or whatever you like,
you're not talking your way out of this. Neither are you
going to shut me out, tease me or ignore me. I'm coming
and that's final, so if you and your sister are ready, *I* will
drive you home, *I* will take care of you and *I* will remain
in charge throughout the night. Do you understand?' She
stood with her hands on her hips, silently daring him to
contradict her.

Stephen didn't break eye contact as he mumbled, 'I
would have kept the oxygen mask on if I'd known I was
going to be subjected to this.'

Nicolette smiled, a smug, feminine smile, and said the
words no man ever liked to hear but which every woman
relished saying. 'I told you so.'

For the second time that night Nicolette drove Stephen's
car. She'd packed a salbutamol inhaler, among other
things, with Stephen specifically in mind. She had definitely discovered more about him in the past few hours.
He was stubborn, egotistical and arrogant, but what man

wasn't? she rationalised. She only hoped he wouldn't oppose her if he needed to take any medicine.

Thankfully, after her spiel in the tearoom, he hadn't said anything more on the subject. Instead, he'd collected his sister and handed over the keys to his car without protest. Now he was sitting in the back seat, holding Stephanie's hand.

'My house,' Stephanie moaned as they drove back to Blackheath.

'Shh.' He brushed her curls out of her face and kissed her forehead. 'We'll work it out. You can stay with me.'

'No.'

'Steph. It's logical. I have the room and we were going to set one up anyway.'

'OK, but only for a few weeks.'

'We can talk about it later. Just rest now.'

'Stephen's right,' Nicolette said. 'Once you're both settled, I'll collect some clothes from my house—we're the same size, Steph, so that's covered.'

'Oh, my clothes!' Stephanie whimpered. 'And my shoes.'

'We'll buy some more,' Stephen murmured. 'It'll be fine, Steph. We're here, we're together. That's what matters.'

All Nicolette's annoyance and frustration towards him melted away in that one instant. He loved his sister, that was very evident, and she remembered what Simone had said about him—that he was callous and incapable of caring for anyone but himself. She needed no further proof that Simone hadn't understood Stephen at all.

She thought back to the way he'd felt so sick, feeling Stephanie's pain, but as they'd closed the distance between the two of them Stephen had become stronger. He was still being strong now but underneath he was vulnerable.

Nicolette pulled the car into his driveway and, using his keys, opened the front door. She waited for Stephen to help his sister in. 'You get her comfortable,' she said, realising the twins needed some time alone. 'I'll be back shortly.'

Stephen met her gaze, frowning. 'I thought we weren't allowed out of your sight.'

Nicolette shook her head slightly. 'Sorry. I overreacted. It's been a tense night for all of us but mostly for Stephanie. Get her settled. I'll be back soon.' As she turned to leave, Stephen reached out and placed his hand on her arm. Nicolette turned back.

'Thanks.' His tone was sincere yet had a hint of surprise. He squeezed her arm before letting her go and returning his attention back to his sister. Nicolette walked back to his car feeling…accepted. As she drove the few short blocks between their houses, she realised she'd been well and truly accepted by Stephen. It was an amazing feeling and one which she felt bound her closer to him. Acknowledging that was a little scary but extremely powerful at the same time.

She knew how close brother and sister were and appreciated that, and it seemed Stephen was willing for her to be a part of it. How on earth was she supposed to fight her growing feelings for the man when he made her feel so special?

When she pulled into her own driveway, she retrieved her keys from the glovebox and headed inside.

Even though her house was cold, she quickly dealt with things, packing clothes into a bag, trying to decide what Stephanie might like to wear. Although they were the same size, they had completely different tastes as far as clothing went. Nevertheless, you could never go wrong with jeans and a woollen jumper. She found an extra toothbrush and packed it along with her own. Stephen would have to take his sister shopping tomorrow for the bare essentials if nothing else.

Nicolette frantically tried to think of what else they might need and then remembered she had to work in the morning. Stephanie might have been given two days off by the hospital director and Stephen could certainly take time out from renovating, but she still had to go to work. She grabbed a two-piece suit, top and shoes from her cupboard, adding them to the pile.

Ten minutes later she turned back into Stephen's driveway and garaged his car. She'd popped open the boot to get her things when he came outside. He'd showered and changed his clothes, and although he was most probably warm she didn't want him breathing in the cold air.

'Go back in.' Her tone was stern and bossy. 'It's cold out here and I don't want you getting worse.'

'I'm fine,' he insisted as he grabbed her bag. 'Your pillow?' He raised his eyebrows.

'I can't sleep without it. It's a special pillow,' she defended herself.

'Hmm. Did it make it to the war zone?'

'Yes.'

'Really?'

She smiled. 'No, of course not, but I missed it the whole time.'

Stephen returned her smile and she had an instant feeling that things were going to work out fine. It had been an extremely tense couple of hours but hopefully they'd all be able to unwind and get things into better perspective.

'How's Stephanie?'

'She's just getting out of the shower. Did you bring a hair drier?'

'Yes.'

'Hmm.'

'And, no, I didn't take that to the war zone either.'

His smile increased. 'Funny. Steph said you'd bring one.'

'So? Is that a bad thing? I have work in the morning.' She picked up her suit where she'd carefully laid it out on the back seat. 'I'll need to do my hair.'

He shook his head. 'Women.'

'What?' she demanded as she gathered the last few things and locked the car.

'Nothing. It's just been a long time since I've lived with a female. I'd forgotten about all the paraphernalia you lot have lying around.'

Stephen headed into the house and Nicolette tried very hard not to let his words get to her. *Lived with a female!* Jealousy stabbed at her and she just stood there, staring at his retreating back, unable to believe she felt the way she did.

He turned. 'What are you doing? Are you coming in or are you going to stay outside and become a snowman?'

She snapped out of it. 'I'm coming.' Why was his comment bothering her so much? As she closed the front door behind her, she remembered that in the war zone it was sometimes necessary for men and women to share the sparse accommodation.

Stephanie walked into the room, wrapped in a huge fluffy towel. Nicolette closed her eyes for a second, amazed at the way her thoughts had gone haywire at Stephen's offhand remark. He had a sister! Duh! He'd grown up with a female, which would account for his words.

'Hey.' Nicolette crossed to her side. 'Feeling better?'

'A bit. Did you bring some clothes?'

'Yes.'

'Hairdryer?'

'Yes.' Nicolette smiled as her thoughts came full circle. 'Stephen has the bag with the clothes. I packed a few sets of pyjamas but help yourself to whatever you need. I also found a new toothbrush.'

Stephanie came forward and hugged her friend. 'Thank you,' she whispered in her ear.

'You're more than welcome. Come on, let me find somewhere to hang my clothes for tomorrow and then we can get his slumber party organised.'

Stephanie smiled at her words. 'Slumber party. Good idea. I'll just pretend I'm having a slumber party.'

The only place Nicolette found to hang her work clothes was Stephen's wardrobe. It felt strange and decidedly intimate to have her suit hanging next to one of his, but she told herself not to be ridiculous. His bedroom seemed to be the only room in the house properly painted and decorated, at least from what she'd seen as she'd walked through.

The walls were a relaxing gumleaf green colour, the ceiling off-white. The timber-framed bed in the middle of the room was the largest she'd ever seen. A matching wooden wardrobe and chest of drawers were against two walls and the whole room had a highly masculine feel. It was so Stephen—and she loved it.

Nicolette left Stephanie to take her pick of the clothes and went in search of Stephen. This was the first time she'd been inside his house and it appeared he had as much work to do here as he had next door. She found him in the large living room, the slow combustion fire burning and rapidly heating the room. He was standing, looking down into the orange glow of the flames as though mesmerised by them.

'You OK?' He turned quickly and she realised she'd startled him. 'Sorry.'

'How's Steph?'

'She's getting dressed.'

'Thanks for lending her some clothes.'

Nicolette shrugged. 'That's what friends are for.'

Stephen nodded. 'You are a good friend.'

A smile touched her lips. 'Know me that well, hey?'

'Better than I did this morning.'

She rubbed her arms and walked over to warm herself by the fire. 'It certainly has been a *long* day.'

'I think I aged an extra twenty years going into that fire.' His words were soft and Nicolette couldn't help but reach out to him. Taking his hand in hers, she squeezed it gently. There was no need for words because between them was an unspoken understanding. Putting your life on the line every day was something they'd both been through and once more, Stephen had lived through those emotions today.

They stayed there for a few minutes, just holding hands and looking into the fire. There was nothing romantic about the touch, just two people who understood each other, and Nicolette could feel the tension slowly leaving him. It was human contact and it was an important part of medicine. Just a reassuring touch to someone's shoulder or an understanding squeeze of the hand could make all the difference and let the person know they weren't alone.

'What do you want to do about the sleeping arrangements?' Stephen eventually asked. 'The spare room is full of boxes and paint tins.'

Nicolette reluctantly dropped his hand and turned to

survey the room. 'This room will be by far the warmest in the house, and both you and Stephanie need to make sure you don't breathe in cold air tonight. What type of heating do you have for the rest of the house?'

'Gas, but it's not the best and I'd rather not risk it.'

'No. That's the last thing we'd all need. OK, so it's this room.' She pointed to the two lounges, which were facing each other. 'Are they comfortable?'

'To sit on, yes, and both are sofa beds as far as I know. They were only delivered last week.'

They each crossed to a lounge and checked beneath the cushions. 'This one is,' Nicolette reported.

'And this one, too.'

'Good. Then I suggest we rearrange your furniture and pull them both out.'

'I'll do that. Why don't you check on Steph?'

Nicolette agreed and headed back to Stephen's bedroom. She knocked on the door and when she heard sobbing on the other side she quickly went in to find her friend, dressed in track pants and sweater, curled up in a ball in the middle of her brother's bed.

'Oh, Steph.' She offered comfort, letting her friend cry. When all the tears were spent, Nicolette looked up from where she'd been sitting on the edge of the bed to find Stephen in the doorway.

'I've made up one of the beds. Let's move her now before she falls asleep.'

'Might be too late.'

Stephen came into the room and Nicolette let go of Stephanie's hand, standing to move out of the way. With what seemed like effortless ease he scooped his sister off the bed, whispered to Nicolette to grab a few pillows and walked out of the room, being careful not to bang Stephanie's head on the doorframe.

Stephen placed Stephanie on the sofa bed and pulled the covers up around her, planting a gentle kiss on her forehead before he straightened. 'She'll sleep through the night.'

'But how do you know—?' Nicolette stopped and nodded. 'She's relaxed?'

'Very. Let's get something to eat, then we can both turn in, too.'

Nicolette glanced across at the other sofa bed and then back to Stephen. He seemed to be inside her head because he said, 'I'll take that one and you can sleep in my bed.'

'Uh, but—'

'My doctor has ordered that I sleep in a warm room.'

Nicolette looked down at the floor. 'That's right, I did. I just feel horrible, kicking you out of your own bed.'

Stephen shrugged as he walked out of the living room. 'It's just for one night. It won't hurt.' He headed to the kitchen, firmly pushing any thoughts of Nicolette curled up in his huge bed from his mind. It was the most logical solution and that's all there was to it. 'Tea and toast?' he asked as she followed him.

'Thanks.' She took in the décor of the room as he filled the kettle and retrieved a loaf of bread from the fridge. 'Interesting colour scheme.'

'I was actually thinking about leaving the orange, brown and purple swirling wallpaper up and just replacing the benchtops, but Steph has convinced me otherwise.'

'Thank goodness.' Nicolette chuckled. 'It really is 1970s, isn't it.'

'The wallpaper, yes, but the house is a lot older than that, but, then, you'd know that because you used to come to Blackheath with your family when you were a girl.'

She smiled. 'Yes, I did. Wow. A man who listens when a woman talks.'

'I resent that comment for my entire sex.' Stephen coughed a little. 'What would you like on your toast?'

'Jam, please.' She eyed him warily, waiting for him to cough again. She continued to watch his every move as he shifted around the cramped kitchen, preparing their supper. 'So what are you going to do with the kitchen?'

'Rip it out.'

'Completely remodel it?'

'Yes.'

'Will you do it yourself or get someone to do it for you?' Stephen shrugged as he took the sugar down and scooped some into both cups of tea. 'Uh, I don't have sugar in tea.'

'You are tonight. The last thing Steph and I need is for our doctor to go into delayed shock.'

'I'm fine.'

'Drink it.' He pushed the cup and plate of toast towards where she stood. 'I might do parts of the kitchen myself. Naturally, I'd get the professionals in to do the plumbing and electricity but I've been known to wield a hammer from time to time.'

'Orthopaedics?' Nicolette took a sip of the sickly sweet tea and then had a bite of her toast.

'There was quite a bit of it in the field but, no, that's not what I meant.' He coughed again. 'I built the furniture in my bedroom.'

That's twice, she thought, but continued with their conversation. 'Really?' Nicolette was highly impressed. 'When?'

'While I was at medical school. I had it in storage for the past few years while I was out of the country so it's nice to finally have it back. I'd forgotten how big I'd made the bed.' He smiled as he began to eat.

'It's huge. However did you find a mattress to fit it?'

'I had it made.'

'Of course you did.' She asked him a few more questions about the art of making furniture as they ate and drank, and after he'd rinsed and stacked their cups and plates, he coughed once more.

'Three strikes, you're out,' she stated, and left the room. She came back a moment later with the salbutamol inhaler and her stethoscope. 'Lift your shirt up, please.'

'Pardon?'

'You heard. I want to listen to your chest.' When he didn't move, she put the stethoscope in her ears and moved closer.

'I'm fine.'

'I'll be the judge of that.'

'I thought you might have forgotten.'

'Would you?'

'No.'

'Then stop insulting my intelligence.' She held out the bottom end of the stethoscope. 'Lift your shirt, please,' Nicolette repeated. This time he did as he was told. She listened closely, closing her eyes, desperately trying not to breathe in his fresh, masculine scent. The close proximity was starting to make her own heart race and she forced herself to concentrate harder.

'You're a little tight.' Was that her voice sounding so husky? She shifted around him, being careful not to touch him except with the medical instrument, as she listened to his back. 'The wheeze is definitely there but mild.' She cleared her throat and moved away, reaching for the inhaler. She held it out him. 'Two puffs of this.'

Stephen eyed the inhaler with disgust. Nicolette took another step back, hoping the distance would ease the overwhelming attraction she felt for him. She was treating him, she was his doctor, she needed to be professional.

'Don't you know how to use one?' she asked in her best no-nonsense tone.

'Of course I do. I don't need to take it.'

'I'm not asking you to take it, Stephen, I'm telling you.'

He shook his head and took it from her. Once he'd finished, he handed it back.

'Now, was that so hard? If you'd been a good boy and done as you were told the first time, you would have received a treat.'

'I *was* good,' he complained.

'Oh?' Nicolette raised her eyebrows. 'Really? If that was good, I'd hate to see you when you're bad.'

'Actually...' He paused for a moment, his gaze meeting hers. 'I think you'd like it.'

CHAPTER SIX

NICOLETTE'S eyes widened at Stephen's words and her jaw dropped open.

'Huh!' The word was said with a mixture of disbelief and repressed desire.

'Sorry.' His cute little smile was back in place, which only continued to create more havoc within her. 'Couldn't resist teasing you a little, especially as you were in your prim and proper doctor mode.'

She didn't feel at all prim and proper now. In fact, her heart was racing, she felt as though she were about to hyperventilate and if she didn't find a chair soon, she'd probably end up collapsing in a heap at his feet. Now that he'd mentioned being bad, she realised he was right—she probably would like him in that mood, especially if being bad meant she'd get more of those delicious kisses they'd shared earlier.

She closed her mouth and looked away, working hard on controlling her breathing. 'OK, then.' Come on, girl. Get it together. 'I'll…um…be checking on you both during the night, but hopefully the salbutamol will help you get a good night's sleep.'

'I doubt it,' he mumbled.

'Pardon?' Nicolette glanced up, unsure she'd heard him correctly.

'Nothing.' They stood there, neither moving, their gazes locked. They were having a conversation but not one that included words. Didn't Nicolette have any idea just how desirable she was? Not only had she been plaguing his thoughts for the past few days; not only did she understand his past experiences; not only did the memory of her mouth on his electrify him—but she somehow smelt totally addictive.

He was insane to let her sleep in his bed because, regardless of how many times he changed the sheets, he knew he would never be able to rid it of her alluring scent. At least he wouldn't have the image of her lying in the bed to contend with because he planned to stay in the living room. He would focus on monitoring his sister and keeping as far away from Nicolette as he possibly could.

With superhuman effort, Stephen looked away. 'I put clean sheets on the bed whilst Steph was in the shower and there are spare towels in the bathroom.'

'Thanks.' Nicolette picked up her stethoscope and the inhaler before shuffling backwards out of the kitchen. 'I'll just check on Stephanie and then turn in.' Without waiting for him to reply, she quickly went to the living room.

Thankfully, her other patient was far more co-operative and she listened to Stephanie's easy breathing, glad her chest seemed clear. She pulled out the other sofa bed but wasn't sure where to find the linen. Stephen walked in, his arms loaded with clothes, linen and pillows.

'Do you want help, making the bed?' She gestured to the sofa bed.

'I'm fine. I've done two tonight, one more won't hurt.'

'Uh, OK.' The awkwardness was starting to settle over them again. 'What about the fire? Can I put another log on?'

'It's fine. I'll stoke it up. There's an alarm clock by the bed if you want to set it for work tomorrow.'

'Thanks.' Oh, they were being so formal, so polite. Why wasn't he making any move to kiss her again? She was sure it was what they both wanted and he'd certainly had ample opportunity. His arms were still cradling the stuff he'd brought out, as though he needed it for protection against her.

'I'll be fine,' he said, and she realised he wanted her gone.

Nicolette forced a smile. 'Goodnight, then.' She headed out of the room, not stopping until she'd entered his bedroom and shut the door behind her. Oh, this was not good, this was *not* good. Stephen obviously didn't want to kiss her again and she started to wonder why. Had it just been a moment of weakness, especially after the stress he'd been through? No. He'd almost kissed her *before* they'd gone to rescue Stephanie, so why hadn't he wanted to repeat it?

'Stop.' Nicolette walked over to her bag of clothes and pulled out a set of comfortable warm pyjamas. 'Don't go down this track again. It happens every time you get interested in a guy and then you end up hurt. Haven't you learnt your lesson at all?' She took a deep breath and closed her eyes for a moment. 'He kissed you, it was fantastic but that's it. That's where it ends. You're colleagues and that's it.'

Nicolette took her clothes and went to the door. She opened it a little to check Stephen wasn't around then quickly went across the hall to the bathroom. After a very quick shower she changed for bed and brushed her teeth. There was no need to check on her patients again and if she did, she'd just be inviting another awkward moment with Stephen.

She returned to his room and set the alarm, not for the morning but to wake her up in an hour's time so she could check on them. Nicolette took the torch she'd packed out of her bag and placed it on the bedside table. Then she stopped and admired the furniture in the room. The bed frame, the wardrobe and dresser and bedside tables. She reached out and touched a hand lovingly to the wood, marvelling at Stephen's skill.

If this was how he worked with wood, she couldn't wait to see his paintings. She could just imagine the intricate detail in his work, the same detail he brought to every-thing he did, whether it was treating a patient, painting a room or…or kissing. Yes, he certainly focused on detail when he was kissing.

She must get that thought out of her head.

Nicolette left the bedroom door open, not only to let some heat into the room but to make it easier when she needed to check on her patients. She climbed under the covers, pulling her own pillow into place, feeling glad she'd brought it as Stephen had snagged all but two throw cushions for himself and Stephanie.

It wasn't hard to get comfortable when she had so much room to spread out, and she forced herself not to think romantically of her present reality—that she was sleeping in Stephen's bed. This was where he slept every night, in this bed which he'd carefully and painstakingly made. She pushed the thought from her mind and closed her eyes, only then realising just how tired she was.

What seemed like only a few minutes later the alarm beeped and Nicolette was surprised to find an hour had indeed passed. She yawned and picked up her torch, pad-ding quietly out to the living room. Thankfully, Stephen was asleep and she listened carefully to them both breathing. His natural breathing was sure and steady so she left them alone and went back to bed, setting the alarm for another hour hence.

After her third trip out she allowed herself to sleep for two hours, satisfied with the status of both her patients.

She climbed back beneath the covers, too tired to control her thoughts, and allowed memories of Stephen's kisses to flow freely.

Stephen woke, unsure where he was for a moment. He lay still as he took in his surroundings and then he remembered everything. He sat up and checked his sister, kissing her forehead when he realised she was still deep in sleep and breathing normally. Next he checked the fire to ensure they stayed warm.

He walked to the kitchen and had a drink of water before grabbing a torch to find where Nicolette had left the salbutamol inhaler. He took two more puffs as his chest felt a little tight again. Then, as though drawn by some invisible force, he found himself heading up the hallway towards his bedroom. He knew he shouldn't do it, and he knew the image of Nicolette in his bed would remain imprinted on his mind for ever, but he *had* to see her. He told himself he was checking on her to make sure she was sleeping OK. After all, she, too, had had a stressful evening.

He also knew he was lying to himself. He wanted to see what she looked like in his bed.

The door was open and the heavy curtains he'd put up yesterday were closed to keep out as much cold as possible. Although the fire had taken the chill out the air, he was surprised at how much colder it was in here compared to the living room, where he'd been sweltering.

Stephen flicked on the torch, quietly walked over to the bed and peered down. He frowned, unable to see her. He looked over his shoulder. Was she up? He listened. No. No sounds. He looked at the bed again and the next instant he saw the covers move. She looked tiny in his bed.

He could just see her now, her blonde hair peeking out from the top of the dark blue doona as she slept on her special pillow. She looked about eighteen years old and totally vulnerable. Her breathing was calm and he knew he should go…but he couldn't.

He stood there, trying to figure out how this woman had become so important to him in such a short space of time yet when he thought about it, how well did he know her? Red warning flags had been waving in his subconscious throughout the day…warnings that she was getting too close, that she was breaking down his barriers.

But had that stopped him from kissing her? No. Stephen shook his head, unable to believe just how mesmerised he was by her. He'd given in to the overwhelming desire to feel her mouth against his—something he'd been wanting to do all day long—and he hadn't been disappointed. In fact, he'd wanted to kiss her again and again and again, and each time he had that urge, another flag went up. She was getting too close.

He needed to leave. Now! He knew that, it was the logical thing to do, but he couldn't move. She looked so incredibly vulnerable, lying there sleeping. Had she thought the same thing when she'd checked on him?

He needed to leave. The words repeated themselves in his mind and this time he forced himself to shift back from the bed. Before he left he checked the alarm clock to see if she'd remembered to set it. The last thing she needed in the morning was to be late for work. He frowned when he saw the time she'd set. Four o'clock!

Stephen realised she'd set the time so she could go and check on himself and Steph, but as it was almost four now and he'd just done the check himself, he changed the setting to half past six. That should give her plenty of time to get ready for work, have breakfast and drive to Katoomba. At least she could get a few extra hours' uninterrupted sleep.

Nicolette shifted again and he held his breath, not wanting her to wake up and find him there. Not only because he might startle her but because he didn't think he'd be able to resist her when she was all tired and mussed up as he knew she would be. It had been bad enough trying to resist her last night, but as he'd told himself over and over, a romantic relationship had no place in his life right now. He was in the middle of making one of his dreams come true—owning his own medical practice. He didn't need complications in the form of a blonde bombshell.

Speaking of blonde, from the way she'd shifted, her hair was lying spread out on the pillow and the urge to touch it was extreme. Stephen reached out, tenderly letting his fingertips touch the soft strands before he pulled away. The tightening in his gut was another warning signal and he was a man who listened to his instincts. Now, though, he found it almost impossible to turn away from her. She was beautiful, no doubt about it, and his reaction was becoming such as he'd never experienced before. Uncharted territory. That was where he was finding himself and he didn't like it one bit.

Stephen closed his eyes for a moment, concentrating on how soft her hair had felt, the way the subtle perfume he was coming to associate with her wound its way about him, making his breathing grow shallow. It wouldn't take much just to bend down and press a kiss to her cheek, but he knew if he did he wouldn't be able to stop. That was something else he didn't like.

Opening his eyes, he dropped his hand and took two huge steps back, glad the carpet masked his footsteps. Before he could think any more, he turned and headed out of the room, strongly berating himself. Not only would he have the image of her sleeping curled up in his bed but now he knew how soft and silky her hair was.

You're being drawn deeper into enemy territory, he warned himself as he climbed onto the sofa bed again, doubting that Nicolette was really his enemy. He'd been through far worse experiences than being attracted to a colleague, but he wondered whether this time it might be fatal.

The alarm went off and Nicolette put her hand out to quickly silence it. She sat bolt upright, disorientated for a second before she realised where she was and what she had to do. Grabbing her torch, she headed out to the living room to check on her patients but stopped dead when she got there.

The light was on and Stephanie was sitting up, sipping a cup of coffee, and the other sofa bed had been packed away, the linen folded neatly. There was no sign of Stephen.

'Where is he?' She blurted the words out and her friend smiled.

'He's just gone outside to get more wood.'

Nicolette crossed to her friend's side, picking up the stethoscope as she went. 'How are you feeling?'

'Much better. My over-protective brother has already listened to my chest.'

'Then you can humour your over-protective friend and let me have a listen, too.' Nicolette hooked the stethoscope into her ears and was glad when Stephanie obliged. 'Good. Nice and clear.' She looked at the bruises and scratches on Stephanie's arms and legs. 'You're going to have some good colour representation here,' she joked.

'You're telling me. I did a good job, that's all I can say.'

'You don't hurt anywhere else?'

'Not physically.'

Nicolette nodded in understanding. To lose all your belongings was devastating.

'It's not just the clothes and shoes and things that upsets me but my photographs, my knick-knacks, my books.' Tears filled Stephanie's eyes and Nicolette hugged her. 'I know I'll get through it. I know I'll bounce back. I'm an optimist and I have people like you and Stephen who care about me, but right now it's just so hard.'

Nicolette squeezed her eyes closed, trying to hold back on her own tears and when she opened them, she looked at the clock on the wall. 'A quarter to seven!' She pulled away from Stephanie. 'That can't be the time. I set the alarm for four so I could check on you, but I don't remember it going off.'

'I changed it.' The deep voice came from behind her and she spun around to see Stephen standing there, fully dressed, his arms loaded with firewood.

'What? Why?'

'Because you needed the sleep just as much as Steph and I did. Besides, I was up just before four, checked on Steph and took some more salbutamol so there was no reason for you to get up to do a four a.m. check.' He put the firewood down and shoved his hands into his jeans pockets.

Nicolette forced herself to take a breath and relax. 'OK. Well, I guess I'd better get ready for work.' She felt a little self-conscious standing in front of Stephen in her pj's while he was wearing hiking boots, black denim jeans and another great fleecy jumper. His cheeks were mildly pink from the chill outside and once more the sight of him got her blood pumping out of control.

Her heart rate picked up the rhythm and her breathing followed suit. As she shifted, she overbalanced and would have fallen back onto Stephanie if Stephen hadn't reached out and grabbed her flailing hand. She jerked away from his touch the instant she was steadier on her feet.

'Thanks.' The word was brisk and it didn't sound as though she was thankful at all. Without looking at either of them, she raced from the room back to the sanctuary of Stephen's bedroom, but even that didn't bring much relief. The need to get out of his house—and *fast*—overwhelmed her. Quickly gathering her toiletries and work clothes, she headed for the bathroom.

Half an hour later she emerged, feeling more in control. She packed her things, leaving clothes for Stephanie, and carried her bag to the front door.

'Leaving before breakfast?' Again, his deep voice washed over her and she took a long breath in, drawing on all her reserves to get her through the next few minutes. She turned to face him.

'Yes. I need to stop by my house before going to work.' She forced a smile. 'Thank you for your hospitality.'

'You're welcome, but you insisted on staying here, from what I can recall.'

'It was necessary,' she snapped, her eyes darkening with impatience. Nicolette looked away and shook her head. 'Sorry, Stephen.'

'Don't apologise. I shouldn't goad you when you've been up and down all night, nursing us back to health.'

'I'd hardly call it that.'

'You forced me to take the salbutamol. Until you did, I honestly didn't think I needed it, but I was surprised at how much relief I gained from it. I took some more at four o'clock.'

'So you said.'

'I was very good. Didn't even whinge about it.' His gaze was quite serious as it met hers. 'I guess I don't get a treat for that.'

'No. The offer has expired.' Again, they were having a completely different conversation with their bodies and minds than with the words they were speaking.

Stephen nodded. 'Very wise.'

'I'll just say goodbye to Stephanie and then head off.'

'I'll get my keys.'

'No!' The word was wrenched from her. 'I'll walk. It's not that far.'

'Nicolette, it's freezing out there.'

She looked down at the ground. '*Ce n'est pas bon,*' she mumbled, then, taking a deep, calming breath, she met his gaze once more. 'I'm fine. Thank you for the offer but I need to go.' She brushed passed him and went in search of Stephanie.

Why wasn't it good? Stephen wondered as he translated her mumbled French. The fact that she had to walk home—or the fact that she was fighting the attraction between them as hard as he was? He dragged some air into his lungs at the thought, excited at the prospect that it was mutual but at the same time knowing it would be a mistake. Fighting the attraction was the right and only thing to do if they were both to remain happy and emotionally unscathed.

Nicolette returned a moment later, shrugging into her coat and tying her scarf.

'Don't forget your gloves,' he murmured, picking them up off the floor where they'd fallen from her coat pocket.

'Thanks.' Her smile was strained. She picked up the bag and reached for the doorhandle. 'I've left a few things for Stephanie on your bed. I hope you don't mind.'

'Not at all. I appreciate the help you've given her.' They were so polite it was almost comical. 'Don't slip on the icy ground.'

'I won't.' Nicolette had never been more relieved to

leave a place. She walked down the drive and crossed the road, her mind replaying over and over the moments they'd just shared. What would she have done if he'd grabbed her and kissed her? She would have kissed him back, of course. That was why she couldn't risk him driving her home. The intimacy of the car would only heighten the feelings between them and they both needed to be strong. The brisk morning air swirled around her, not only waking her up but also helping to cool the rising passion she felt for Stephen.

Personally, the last thing she needed was to get romantically involved with someone she was hoping to work closely with in the near future. She needed to be professional because she'd learnt from bitter past experience that business and pleasure just didn't mix.

It wasn't hard to avoid Stephen for the next two weeks, although every time she saw Stephanie she would listen intently when his sister mentioned his name.

Stephanie had bounced back, as she'd said she would, and after spending a week with Stephen had moved into a house owned by a friend who lived in Sydney.

'He usually rents it out when he's not here, but as the estate agent hasn't contacted him to say it has a tenant, he said I could use it for as long as I wanted.'

'Excellent.'

'It's only a block from where I was before so I'm still close to the hospital.'

'I'm really happy for you.' Nicolette sipped her coffee. 'How's the clothes shopping going?'

'Very good, actually. Stephen drove me down to Sydney for two days and I shopped until I dropped. It was very therapeutic.'

'Is that when you had the, um, colour put through your hair?' Nicolette laughed as she spoke.

'You don't like bright green?' Stephanie ran her fingers over her three millimetres of hair, which was indeed bright green.

'It's so...*you*.'

'Thank you and also thanks for your donation. We raised heaps of money in our "Shave for a Cure" campaign.'

'You're more than welcome. Giving money was easy as I'm nowhere near as brave as you.'

Stephanie laughed and Nicolette realised it was good to see her friend so cheerful again. 'You're not the only person who's said that to me.' Stephanie's pager beeped. 'Ugh,' she groaned after checking the number. 'It's hospital admin. I'll bet they want to discuss next week's rosters.'

'When does the new director arrive?'

'Saturday and I can't wait. This will be the last time I have to do those horrible rosters.'

Nicolette nodded and took another sip of her coffee. She was almost one hundred per cent sure Stephen had asked his sister not to roster himself and *her* together for their stints at the hospital because she hadn't worked with him for the past two weeks. She wasn't sure whether she was glad or disappointed so she forced herself to think of something else.

Nothing more had been said to her about his practice and she wondered whether he'd changed his mind about working with her. She knew, if she officially accepted the position, it would mean seeing him every day and she'd been building up her confidence to cope with that. The fact of the matter was, thoughts of him still plagued her dreams and she'd woken every morning since the fire at

Stephanie's house eager to have Stephen's lips pressed to hers once more. It was ludicrous.

'Anyway, it was great catching up for coffee,' Stephanie said as she swallowed the rest of her drink and stood. 'I'd better get back to the hospital and see what Admin wants.'

'OK. Want to meet next week again?'

'Sure. Oh, I almost forgot.' She withdrew a large envelope from her briefcase and handed it over. 'Stephen asked me to give this to you. He was going to drop it off at the hospital but I told him I'd be seeing you first so you can just call me courier girl.'

Nicolette took the envelope, her palms instantly perspiring. 'Er…thank you, courier girl.' She turned it over, not sure she wanted to open it. 'What is it?'

'It's not a ticking time bomb which is obviously what you think from the look on your face. It's your employment contract.'

'Oh.' So he *was* willing to go through with it.

Stephanie wound her scarf around her neck and pulled on her gloves. 'Can I give you some advice?'

'Uh…sure.' Nicolette frowned, wondering what her friend was going to say as she'd gone all serious.

'Don't let your past dictate your future.'

'Pardon?'

'When you first came to the Blue Mountains, you told me about your failed relationships, remember?'

'Yes.'

'You said none of those guys really understood you, and you were probably right—they didn't. I know you've worked in a war zone and Stephen mentioned you'd had discussions about it so you've obviously opened up to each other. You understand what he's been through. Getting my head shaved is nothing compared to what both of you must have faced. I have no idea what life was like there and I don't want to know. The sleepless nights I had, the pain I felt when Stephen got shot—'

'He got shot?' Nicolette was surprised he hadn't mentioned that. Then again, it wasn't that easy to talk about, but surely he'd have realised when they'd been swapping stories that she, of all people, would have understood. Then again, perhaps he didn't know that.

'It was a flesh wound but, boy, did it hurt. I think I got most of the pain. I could barely move my arm for days. Anyway, I can only empathise with what he's been through but you've seen it all at first-hand and that gives you two a bond. A *strong* bond. I've seen the way you are with each other and the fact that you're attracted to each other is quite clear.'

'It is?'

'To *me*,' Stephanie clarified quickly. 'When you two are together, Stephen…he—'

'You feel him,' Nicolette interjected.

'Yes, but it's like nothing I've felt before. It's quite strange really.' Her pager beeped again and she shook her head. 'I'm coming,' she told the inanimate object. 'I'd better give them a call so they know I'm on my way.' She checked her cellphone. 'No signal. No wonder they're paging me. Sorry. I really have to go, but all I'm saying is, don't let your past dictate your future. If you think there's something real between you and Stephen then go for it.'

'But what if I get hurt?'

Stephanie shrugged. 'Then you pick up the pieces of your life and move on with the help of your friends.'

'What about you? You're my friend and his sister. I don't want you to be in the middle.'

Stephanie smiled as she picked up her briefcase. 'Too late for that. I'll call you.'

Nicolette closed her eyes, thinking over Stephanie's words. Could she do it? Did she want to do it? She'd vowed that working with Stephen meant no romantic involvement, but what if it was inevitable? What if they were destined to be together?

She opened her eyes and focused on the envelope. Business. Concentrate on business for a start. She took the papers out and read them. Everything was set out properly and she reached for her pen, signing on the dotted line. She put the papers back in the envelope and shrugged into her coat, deciding to deliver the papers straight back to Stephen so he wasn't left waiting.

Nicolette walked out and climbed into her expensively fixed car, glad to have it back in working order again. She drove to Stephen's house, parked outside and decided to try the clinic first rather than his house. She took a deep breath and slowly exhaled before she knocked firmly on the door. No answer. She tried the handle and the door opened so she went inside.

'Hello?' she called. 'Stephen?'

'Back here,' came his call, and she headed in that direction. The clinic looked very different from the previous time she'd been here. The walls were finished, the carpet was new and there was a reception desk and waiting-room chairs in place. There were even a few little tables here and there with magazines and children's books. In one corner was a pot plant and in the other a toy box. Easy-to-look-at prints were hung on the walls and over the receptionist's desk was a cartoon-character clock. She smiled—no doubt a present from Stephanie.

Nicolette scanned the room as she walked through it, marvelling at the work Stephen had done.

'Hello?' His voice was getting closer and in the next instant he walked into the waiting room. 'Nicolette. I thought it was you.'

'You've done an amazing job, Stephen.' Her eyes were bright with excitement as she smiled. 'I can't believe it's the same place that was covered with ladders and painting paraphernalia the last time I was here.'

He shrugged, more interested in looking at her than the room around him. It had been only a few weeks since they'd last seen each other but it felt like a year. She was dressed in another one of her power trouser suits but this one was a deep burgundy colour which made her appear warm and inviting as well as incredibly sexy. Her hair was pulled back in its usual chignon and her winter coat was hanging open at her sides. Looking at her, it was as though he'd found his oasis after crawling through the scorching desert, and that thought bothered him. 'What can I do for you?'

Nicolette was a little surprised at his gruff tone but shrugged and held the envelope out to him. 'The contract. Signed, sealed and delivered.'

'Thank you.' He took them from her and placed them on the reception desk. They both stood there for a moment, staring at each other, drinking their fill as though it had been far too long—which it had.

He was dressed in his old painting clothes again and she realised, belatedly, she should apologise for interrupting him. 'I'll let you get back to whatever it was you were doing.'

He shrugged. 'Now you're here, come and take a look. You can give me your honest opinion.'

She nodded and followed him down the corridor to where he pointed out the filing room, where shelves had been built to house hard copies of patient files. The kitchen was next, equipped with a table, comfortable chairs, fridge-freezer, large urn and a microwave. 'Cup of tea or coffee?' he offered.

'No, thanks.' She smiled at him. 'I've just had one with your sister.'

'Of course. Down here are the consulting rooms and then the third door at the end is a treatment room for any emergencies that come in.' He took her around the entire place and when they were in the second consulting room he added, 'Feel free to bring in any pictures or things you want. You'll have a computer on your desk—they arrive tomorrow.'

'Great. As I said before, Stephen, it's amazing what you've done.'

'I've discussed the hand-over of patients with Dr River, and it's all set to go ahead at the beginning of next week so I have six more days to finish everything else off and then we're ready for business.'

'Ready for business,' Nicolette repeated with a little smile. 'That's good.' And it was.

'How was clinic today?' he asked, searching for something to say.

'Busy.' She shrugged. 'Dr River can hardly wait to hand over the reins.'

'Looking forward to retirement already?'

'Yes. He was out playing a round of golf today. I don't know how as it was so cold.'

'You've never talked to him much about the practice as such, have you,' Stephen stated.

'No. I'm just a doctor who comes in and works for him, and that's the way it's always been.' Nicolette shrugged. 'Each to their own.'

She seemed so sad and forlorn that a powerful need to protect her surged through him. He had no idea what he was supposed to be protecting her from—except himself, of course. He cleared his throat and said briskly, 'That's not the way this practice will work. You do realise that, don't you?'

'I read the contract, Stephen, and I understand we'll be running the practice together, even though you own it.'

'Total disclosure.'

'Yes.'

'We're a team, Nicolette.'

'You can count on me.'

Stephen watched her closely, then nodded. 'Yes. You've had first-hand experience at how important good communication is.'

'That's right.'

He nodded and smiled. Nicolette instantly wished he hadn't as she was once more lost in the emotions he evoked with his gorgeous smiles.

'Would you like to have dinner tonight?' she blurted out, regretting it the instant the words were out her mouth.

Stephen looked momentarily stunned, his grin disappearing. She shouldn't have said that. Why had she said that? Nicolette silently berated herself but it was too late to take it back.

'You mean…' Stephen said slowly, and she saw the teasing twinkle in his eyes. 'As in a *date*?'

Nicolette laughed and the tension was immediately broken. 'Well…' She shrugged nonchalantly. 'You can call it a date if you like but don't get upset if we start discussing business.'

CHAPTER SEVEN

'WE COULD have taken my car,' Nicolette protested as Stephen turned onto the main street of Blackheath. 'It is fixed now.' She leaned over and put her bag on the back seat, getting it out of the way.

'I know, but I like my car.' Stephen had quickly gone next door to his house and changed into a pair of trousers and comfortable jumper, again making it almost impossible for Nicolette not to want to kiss him senseless. He looked so good and she was happy they were going to spend some time together.

'Are you implying I don't like my car?'

'Do you?' He stopped at the traffic lights, waiting to turn left. They were going to a restaurant in Katoomba which Nicolette had heard was good. She couldn't believe how happy she felt, being with Stephen like this, bickering about nothing. It was…uplifting, especially after the past two weeks which had seemed like crawling across the Nullarbor Plain—dry, parched land with not a tree in sight.

'I like it when it's working,' she replied.

'My point exactly. I like my car more, which means we go in my car.'

Nicolette laughed. 'Are you going to be this impossible at our business meetings?'

He pretended to consider her question thoughtfully before saying simply, 'Yes.'

'Typical male.'

'I hardly think I deserved that comment.'

It was her turn to pretend to give his words consideration. 'Possibly. Prove to me otherwise. I suppose you think of your car as female, too.'

'All cars are female,' he stated matter-of-factly.

'Typical male,' she said again, trying to bite back the giggle bubbling up.

Stephen glared at her with mock indignation and opened his mouth to say something but the light changed.

'It's green. You can go,' she pointed out.

'Saved by the light...for now. Speaking of green, what do you think of my sister's hair?'

Nicolette laughed again, realising just how much she'd missed him. 'Only Stephanie could pull it off so successfully. I think she looks fantastic.'

'I'll admit I was speechless when I picked her up from the hairdresser's. I know I shouldn't have left her unsupervised but she'd dragged me to every clothes shop in the Sydney CBD. I just needed time out and thought she'd be safe at the hairdresser's.'

'You didn't even wonder why she would go to the hairdresser's, especially when her hair was already that short?'

'A fleeting thought passed through my mind when she announced that she'd made an appointment but I confess I was too exhausted to question her. All I could see was an opportunity for me to return to the car with her packages and sit down in peace and quiet.'

'You old man you.'

Stephen glanced across, a smile on his face. He returned his attention to the road and frowned. 'What the...?' They were coming into Medlow Bath, just before the overpass where the road went over the electric train tracks.

Nicolette looked out the front windscreen, her eyes widening in horror. 'The coal truck! It's...' She couldn't get the words out properly. 'The tourist bus!' She reached out a hand as though she could stop the accident from happening, but both of them watched helplessly.

A loud, echoing crack was heard as the coal truck collided with the tourist bus, forcing it off the road. Stephen braked, keeping their distance as best he could. The coal truck was still moving, grinding down the side of the bus. As though in slow motion, they watched as the front of the bus crashed through the guardrail of the railway overpass. For a second the bus teetered before going over completely.

Nicolette felt her mouth go dry and her heart stop for a split second as she witnessed the horror and devastation. In the next instant everything kicked into gear. Stephen pulled to the side of the road and they both flew out of the car, the reverberations of the sound of the bus landing on the train tracks below assailing their ears. A continuous shriek of metal on metal pierced the air before another loud crack was heard.

'What was that?' Nicolette asked, her heart thudding wildly against her ribs. Stephen tossed her his car keys.

'Call it in,' he yelled over the noise. 'Get my medical bag. I'll take a look.'

'Be careful. The overhead train cables may still be live.'

'Good point.'

Nicolette pulled her phone from her pocket and dialled the emergency number, giving as much detail as she could, which wasn't much at this stage. She unlocked the boot of Stephen's car and retrieved his medical bag. She finished speaking and disconnected the call.

The next job was to make sure the traffic didn't come any closer. The cars on the road behind had slowed and almost stopped. She rushed over to the first one and the driver wound down his window.

'What's going on?' he asked.

'I need your help,' she said, motioning for them to get out. 'My colleague and I are doctors and we need your help.'

'B-but I don't know anything,' the man stuttered. She guessed him to be in his early twenties, and even as he took in the scene around them, she could see him going pale. She turned to the woman, who looked about the same age, as she got out of the passenger seat.

'I need you to control the traffic for a start. Get some other people to help you if necessary. Can you do that? We need to keep people clear if they're not injured, and we also need to be able to get emergency vehicles through.'

'We can do that,' the woman said. 'Have you called the police?'

'Yes. Emergency crews have been notified.'

'What do we do if people are feeling sick?' the man asked, still as white as a sheet.

'Get them to sit down. Write down their names and what's wrong with them.' The smell of dust, petrol and another lurid smell she couldn't identify were beginning to fill the air. She needed to get to Stephen. To help him. 'We need people to remain calm and out of the way.'

'I can do that,' the woman said again. 'Come here, Daryl,' she muttered as she grabbed her boyfriend's hand and took him over to the side of the road. 'Sit down and put your head between your knees.'

Nicolette turned away and looked for Stephen. She couldn't see him so headed in the direction he'd gone. As she was walking, she called the hospital to let them know where she and Stephen were but they desperately needed backup.

'I'll call with more info as I get it,' she told Stephanie. At that moment, she saw Stephen. 'Just a second, Steph.'

'A train was just coming into the station,' he said when he was closer. 'That loud crack was the train hitting the coach. It's pushed it along the tracks into the station.'

'God help us,' she whispered in shock. She relayed the information to Stephanie before ending the call. 'Where do we start?'

'You check the driver of the coal truck and I'll head down to the train station. Keep your phone on you so we can communicate.'

'Right.' She handed him the medical kit. 'You take this. The truck driver should have some sort of first-aid kit.'

'Let's hope he does.' Stephen nodded and headed off. Nicolette went over to the truck. The back wheel was right on the edge of the overpass where the bus had crashed through, the front cab up hard against the rail. She walked around to the passenger side, sniffing carefully in case there was a fuel spill.

'Hello?' she called, but received no response. Cars coming from the other direction had stopped and someone was taking care of keeping people away. 'Hello?' she called again, and climbed up the passenger side of the truck. The door was stuck but she could see the driver through the window. He was slumped over the steering wheel, unconscious. She pulled harder on the doorhandle.

'I don't think you should do that, little lady.' A big, burly man had come across. Nicolette looked down at him.

'I'm a doctor. Can you get this door open for me?' She climbed down and he quickly went up and after a few tries managed to force the door open. 'Thanks.' She headed back up and clambered over the seat, pressing two fingers to the driver's carotid pulse. Nothing. She checked to see if he was breathing. Nothing. She moved around so she could see his eyes—they were fixed and dilated.

'Is he all right, Doc?' the man asked.

'No. He's dead.' Nicolette glanced at her watch. 'Seventeen-fifty.' She turned and clambered back the way she'd come. Before she got out, she searched the truck for a first-aid kit or other things she could use and came up trumps. In the glove compartment was a small first-aid kit, which was better than nothing.

'What are you going to do? You can't just leave him there.' The man followed her down to the ground.

'There's nothing I can do for him and the police and forensic department need to deal with him. Get a piece of paper and pen for me, please.' She went to the rear of the truck again and peered over the edge to the devastation below, her gaze searching for Stephen. She couldn't see him. The man returned and she wrote down the details of what she'd found with the truck driver and the time. 'Stay up here and keep things under control,' she told the man. 'Don't let anyone except emergency crews near the coal truck, and when the police arrive, give them this.' She handed over the piece of paper. 'Thanks.'

Nicolette raced along the road to the edge of the guard-rail and then carefully slid down the embankment. She headed back towards the train station, calling Stephen on his phone as she went. 'Where are you?' she asked when he answered.

'At the head of the train. The driver's dead. Killed on impact.'

'Truck driver's dead also. Not sure why. What's happening with triage?'

'I've put the stationmaster in charge. She wasn't too impressed but she'll do fine. I need you.'

'I'm on my way.' Nicolette disconnected the call but a second later the phone rang.

'Nic, it's Steph. What's going on?'

Nicolette gave Stephanie a brief update. 'Go to the bus first. Stephen's in the train, which is where I'm headed.'

'OK.'

Nicolette hung up and continued through the scattered debris to the train station. There, she found it hard to walk past people who needed help, but Stephen obviously had a situation that required her expertise as well as his.

'Stephen?' she called when she neared the head of the train.

'Nicolette?' He didn't sound far away and she kept searching. She found him in the first carriage, the one directly behind the engine. The metal was twisted but the doors had been prised open. Although there were several people still inside, others were helping them out.

'Where are you?' she asked as she stepped onto the train.

'Over here.' He was lying flat on his stomach, his legs sticking out from beneath a part of the metal which had collapsed almost to the floor. 'Be careful. The seats aren't stable so don't lean on them.'

'Acknowledged.'

'Right. Lie down next to me.'

Nicolette made her way carefully towards him and knelt down, placing the first-aid kit on the floor beside her before she removed her jacket. Stephen's medical bag was next to him and she quickly pulled on a pair of gloves before lying flat and sliding under the piece of metal beside him. 'What have we got?' she asked as she lifted her head. The roof hadn't collapsed as far here and she could actually lift her head and shoulders, leaning on her elbows. The only light came from a torch Stephen had jammed in between some fallen metal. She glanced at the patient in front of them, who was trapped and unconscious.

'Approximately fifteen-year-old boy, both legs jammed.' Stephen indicated to where they had been crushed by a seat which had broken away from its mounting. Blood pressure is dropping.' Stephen's portable sphymomanometer cuff was deflated but still wound around the boy's right arm.

Nicolette took the boy's pulse. 'No, not good.' She took Stephen's medical torch and checked the boy's pupils—equal and reacting to light. Good. 'Can you hear me?' No response.

'How long until the first ambulance arrives?'

'Your guess is as good as mine. They have to get through any traffic first.'

'I'm going to need oxygen, plasma and those emergency crews with their handy gadgets to cut him out.'

'What about his legs? His femoral artery might be damaged and that's where he's probably losing the blood. It could take hours to cut him out, Stephen, and he may not have hours,' Nicolette said softly.

'Agreed. This boy's the worst in this carriage, which took the brunt of the impact. The carriage behind isn't internally damaged from what I can see.'

'Right.' She looked back at the boy. 'Do you think we can lift that part of the seat off his legs? That way, you could get a look at them.'

'We're not in a good position to lift. I've tried and I can move it but not lift it.'

'Just a second.' She backed out, shuffling along the floor until she was sure she wouldn't hit her head, then turned around and went in feet first. 'Guide me,' she called, and listened to Stephen's instructions. 'If I can get close enough, I can lift it off with my feet then you can shift him over so you can treat him.'

'Brilliant. Right, come closer, closer.' Stephen guided Nicolette until her feet could reach the seat. 'All right, now shift around towards me, keep your feet in place and bend your knees. Good. Comfortable?'

'Oh, just great,' she mumbled as she concentrated. The twisted roof was only a hair's breadth from her nose. She closed her eyes, which helped, forming a mental picture of what she was doing. With her knees bent and her feet firmly beneath the seat, she pressed her hands palms down onto the floor to help her when she needed to push. 'Am I in position?'

'Almost. A little more to the right. Good. Stop. Ready?'

'Ready.'

'OK. Just let me shift a little so I can reach him more easily.' Nicolette waited for Stephen to be ready. They might only get one chance at this and it needed to work. 'Right. Let's do this. Three, two, one—*lift*.'

Nicolette dragged in a breath and pushed with all her might. She felt the seat move.

'More, more,' Stephen urged. 'That's it. It's working. A little more. Good. Hold it there.'

Nicolette concentrated on keeping her legs in place, already beginning to feel the muscles burning. She breathed in and out, trying to control the urge to rest. 'Stephen,' she called urgently when she felt she couldn't hold it any longer.

'Almost there. You're amazing. Doing a brilliant job,' he encouraged as he stretched to finish moving the boy's legs. It was harder than he'd thought because as he'd stretched he'd also become stuck between the floor and the roof, giving him little room to manoeuvre. 'OK. Five…four…' He knew he had to work fast. She was going to collapse soon. 'Three…two…' There, he'd freed the second leg, the boy's jeans ripping as he finally man-oeuvred the leg out. 'One. Let it down gently. Easy.'

Nicolette gave a strangled cry as she eased up on the pressure, the burning sensation tearing through her. Finally, her legs were on the floor and it was only then she realised she was shaking all over.

'Did you get him?'

'Yes. Just rest.'

Nicolette did as he'd suggested but a minute later her phone rang. She wriggled her backside and then worked her way backwards until finally she was out. Tired and exhausted, she lay there and reached into her trousers pocket for her phone.

'Nic?'

'Stephanie,' she breathed. 'What's up?'

'Oliver wanted me to let you know the paramedics have taken over the triage on the station platform and the health resort down the road has agreed to act as a base for cases until we can get reinforcements here from Springwood. Is Stephen all right?' There was a warning tone in Stephanie's voice and it immediately caused a prickle of apprehension to wash over Nicolette.

'I think so. Stephen,' she called. 'Are you all right?'

'I'm fine. Jammed but fine.'

'He's jammed but fine.'

'That's why I've been feeling as though walls were closing in.'

'Listen, we have a boy here with possible ruptured fem-oral artery. Stephen's taking a look now.' Nicolette gave their location.

'I'll send equipment and personnel down to you.'

'Thanks.' She disconnected the call and lay there, her body still trembling.

'You all right?' Stephen called.

'I just need one more minute.'

'You did an amazing job. Femoral artery is ruptured. I need sutures. Check my medical bag and see if I have some.'

Nicolette grabbed some energy from somewhere and shifted around to check his bag. 'No. You don't have any. Wait a second,' she said as she saw a blur of a white shirt through the cracked window. 'I think the cavalry's arrived.' Nicolette managed to sit up as paramedics came in. 'We're glad to see you, boys.'

'What do you need, Nic?'

'A fresh set of gloves and sutures for a start. Oh, and a pair of scissors wouldn't go astray. I'll go back under and you can pass the equipment to me.' She took the gloves and sutures and lay on her stomach once more. 'Here we go again,' she muttered. 'Are you still jammed, Stephen?'

'Yes, so be careful coming through.'

'Maybe I can shift you over.'

'I'm fine for now and, besides, it's not as though I have anywhere to go.'

Nicolette handed him the sutures and cut away the fabric, which was practically soaked with blood. Stephen was having a close look at the wound sites.

'How bad is it?'

'The right leg is worse. Retract,' he said, and Nicolette used her gloved hands to hold the skin and muscles out of the way so Stephen could do what he needed to do. 'Got it,' he said a moment later.

'Nice going. Let me guess, you've done this before.' Their gazes met and held for a second before Stephen focused on his work.

'You could say that.'

'Lost count of how many busted legs you've fixed?'

'Yes.'

'Me, too. Right, I need to shift to the other side of you so I can do his obs and get the oxygen and drip on him.' Again she wriggled back.

Within another five minutes Nicolette had placed an oxygen mask over the patient's nose and mouth, the long tube reaching back to where the paramedics were. 'Give me a long tube on the IV line as well,' she called. 'I've got nowhere to hang it here.'

Nicolette and Stephen kept calling to their patient but received no response. Nicolette inserted a saline drip into their patient's right arm and splinted the IV line in place. Stephen bandaged the boy's legs as best he could, given the state of the fractures, but at least the bleeding had stopped. 'BP?' she asked as Stephen deflated the cuff once more.

'Better.'

'Good.' Nicolette checked the reading on the oximeter. 'Oxygen sats up to 94 per cent.'

'That's what we want to hear. Now you're in with a fighting chance, lad,' Stephen told their still unconscious patient. 'Pass me the medical torch and I'll do his obs again.'

Nicolette did as he asked then called to the paramedics. 'How long do the emergency crews think it will take to get him out?'

'About another two hours.'

Stephen nodded. 'That's what I thought. Get a bag of plasma ready in case he goes into shock—which, given the circumstances, is on the cards.'

'Will do,' the paramedic called back.

'Can you move or are you still jammed?' Nicolette asked.

'I'm still jammed and it's starting to become annoying.'

'Let's get you unstuck, then. I take it your hips are jammed?'

'Yes. If I can just wriggle to the left and down that should do it, but I'll need a bit of a shove.'

'I need to be on the other side of you.' Nicolette sighed and began shifting backwards. 'You know, I was once stuck in a cave similar to this for about six hours. Enemy fire outside and two dead soldiers for company. It wasn't fun.'

'Doesn't sound like it. Thank goodness you're not claustrophobic.'

'Well, I wasn't after that experience.'

Stephen chuckled then frowned. Nicolette was amazing, and the more he got to know her the more he liked her. He'd stayed away from her for the past two weeks for that simple reason—he honestly didn't have any room for anything new in his life right now. It was full enough.

Now that their patient was stable and the immediate danger had disappeared, this time when she slid in beside him he was acutely aware of exactly how close she was.

'All right. I'm in position. What do you want, boss?'

'Boss? I like the sound of that.'

It was Nicolette's turn to laugh. 'Just give me instructions, you dope.'

'OK. You're going to need to give me a bit of a shove from my waist. Push down and to the side.'

'Gotcha. Ready?'

'Yes.' He counted down and they moved together, Stephen becoming unstuck instantly. 'Thank you.' He cleared his throat, his skin burning with pleasure from where Nicolette had touched him.

'You're most welcome. Right. How's the patient?'

'I'll do the obs, but if he's stable we can leave him to

the paramedics and get back to work.' A minute later both Stephen and Nicolette were finally out from beneath the twisted roof. He helped her to her feet and dropped her hands as soon as she was standing. 'How are your legs?'

'Better. Not as wobbly.'

'Good. I was concerned you'd hurt yourself but thankfully you didn't.' Stephen gave the paramedics instructions before reaching for his phone. 'Steph. What's happening?'

'Your patient stable?' Stephanie asked, and Stephen frowned a little. Something wasn't completely right with his sister, but he wasn't sure what. She felt…different somehow. He put it down to the stressful situation they were all in.

'For now. Where do you need us?'

'Oliver and I are in the bus. The driver has been taken out and is hopefully being airlifted to Sydney as we speak. Three people are dead and another is trapped—between two of the deceased. She's stable for now and the emergency crews are in the process of cutting her out.'

Stephen relayed the information to Nicolette. 'Head to the health resort?'

'Yes. I'll catch up with you soon.'

Stephen disconnected the call and collected his medical bag, putting into it the first-aid kit Nicolette had grabbed. 'Let's go.'

'Who's Oliver?' Nicolette asked as they headed up the platform.

'I have no idea, but you can bet I'll be finding out.'

'You have that protective big-brother attitude about you,' she remarked with a chuckle.

Stephen stopped still and stared at her in astonishment. 'How do you do that?'

'Do what?'

'Read me so easily.' He started walking again, knowing they should be focusing on their work but it was hard when she unnerved him like that. The only woman he was used to having inside his head was his sister. He didn't know if he could deal with another one.

Nicolette shrugged as she fell into step beside him. 'I guess we're on the same wavelength.'

It mirrored his own thoughts of a couple of weeks ago and where he'd thought keeping his distance would help give a clearer perspective on the situation with Nicolette, he realised now he had been wrong. It only served to heighten everything he felt for her, and that would never do.

CHAPTER EIGHT

WHEN they arrived at the health resort, Nicolette looked around at the people gathered there. Taking a breath, she headed into the throng, working through patients one by one.

She hardly saw Stephen for the next few hours but when she stopped for a much-needed cup of coffee, he came over. 'Our trapped boy has been freed,' he told her.

'Excellent. Are they taking him to Sydney?'

'Yes. The urgent cases have all been taken there as the hospitals are better equipped to deal with them.'

'I hope he pulls through. He seemed like a fighter.' She drained her cup.

'Yes, he did.'

'I guess we'd better get back to the patients, although things seem to be settling down now. Katoomba hospital will be bursting at the seams with people needing X-rays or casts. I've lost track of the number of suspected broken bones I've looked at.'

Stephen nodded his agreement. 'At least we're not surrounded by sniper-fire,' he pointed out and Nicolette smiled.

'Ah, the silver lining. I knew there was one here somewhere. Hey, have you met Oliver yet? Quite a dish, if you ask me.'

Stephen's frown was instant. 'Not you, too.' Why did he feel a stabbing sensation around his heart? He pushed it away, desperate to keep his comments light. 'Half the nurses here are swooning over him.'

'Understandable. What about Steph? Is she swooning, too?'

'She can't seem to stand him.'

Nicolette raised her eyebrows. 'Interesting.' She smiled before leaving him with his thoughts. Did this mean Nicolette *wasn't* interested in the new A and E director? He certainly hoped so.

'Stephen, isn't it?' Oliver Bowan came up beside him.

'Yes.' Stephen looked the man over—dark hair, blue eyes. Nothing he could see that was extraordinary. Was it true his sister couldn't stand him or was she simply trying to mask her emotions? Things had been too hectic for him to figure out exactly what Stephanie was feeling. He cleared his throat, slipping instantly into protective big-brother mode.

'If you and Nicolette head back to the hospital and get things sorted out there, that would be good. I can wrap things up here.'

'What about Steph?'

'Stephanie?' Oliver frowned as though trying to figure out who Stephanie was. Surely he knew who she was and if he'd forgotten Stephanie so quickly, why had he remembered Nicolette's name so easily? Was the new A and E director interested in Nicolette? The protective big-brother mode was pushed aside to make way for pure green jealousy.

'Stephanie Brooks. The woman who's been filling in for you?' Stephen said between gritted teeth.

'I know who she is. Yes, she'll be staying to help me finish up.'

'She's an excellent doctor.'

Oliver merely shrugged as though he didn't care one way or the other before heading off. Stephen glared at the man for a few seconds and then went to find Nicolette.

When she'd finished with her patient, he passed on the message.

'Right. I'll write up these notes and then I guess we can head back to your car. Do you have the keys or do I?'

'You had them last.'

She patted her trousers pockets. 'Ah, here they are.' She handed them over and concentrated on what she needed to do, which was easier said than done. Stephen stood beside her, closer than usual, and actually leaned over to see what she was writing. She could feel the warmth emanating from his body and wondered what he would do if she shifted to the left slightly, thereby bringing their bodies into contact with each other. Would he react at all? Probably not. It was probably her exhausted imagination playing tricks on her yet again. She and Stephen had been avoiding each other for the last two weeks so how could he possibly be interested?

'All set,' she said, surprised to find her voice a little husky. 'Where's Stephanie?'

Stephen pointed to where his sister sat beside a boy of about thirteen, letting him touch her spiky hair. Both Nicolette and Stephen smiled. 'Typical Steph,' Stephen murmured.

'I was just thinking the same thing. Is she staying here or do we need to give her a lift?'

'She's staying with Dr Bossy-Britches.'

'Ooh. Juvenile name-calling.' Nicolette's grin was wide. 'I take it you're picking up on your sister's emotions. If he tries to kiss her, are you going to give him a knuckle sandwich?' She chuckled. Stephen's answer was to put his hand beneath her elbow and usher her quickly towards the front door. She just had time to grab her jacket from where she'd draped it over a chair and soon they were out in the freezing night air.

'Well, I guess the brisk walk back to the car should help warm us up,' she said, trying not to focus on the tingles that were currently bursting around her body from his touch. Every time he touched her she had the same reaction, but at least now she'd experienced it a few times she was able to cope better with the intensity of it.

'Excuse me.' A police officer stopped them. 'Did you say you needed to get back to your car?'

'Yes. It's just before the overpass on the Blackheath side,' Stephen replied.

'I'll get you through, Doc. Come with me.'

Nicolette was glad to get into the police car as it shielded her from the bitterly cold wind. The drive didn't take long and she saw that the coal truck had been moved off the road and the emergency crews were working hard to fix the barrier where the coach had gone over.

'There it is.' Stephen pointed to his own car and within another few minutes they were heading to the hospital, the car heater at its highest setting. 'What a night.'

'So much for dinner.'

'Raincheck?' He was surprised with himself. Did he really want to put himself in the position where he'd be sitting across from Nicolette, just the two of them, eating dinner, trying to think of sparkling conversation whilst playing footsie beneath the table? Yes. Absolutely, *yes*! Was that what he'd planned on doing tonight if they'd had their date. He didn't know. His feelings for Nicolette had once again altered over the course of the evening and now he had no idea what he wanted.

The hospital loomed into view and he pushed the thoughts way to the back of his mind. He parked the car and they walked into A and E, trying not to groan as they

were greeted with a similar scene to that at the health
resort. People were everywhere and everyone required attention.

'Ready for round two?' he murmured as they headed
to the changing rooms.

'Ready as I'll ever be.' They both punched in the codes
for their respective rooms and entered. Nicolette had a
quick shower and dressed in theatre scrubs. She usually
didn't like wearing them while she worked but tonight it
was necessary as her own clothes were so dirty.

When she headed out, she found Stephen dressed the
same, his hair damp. 'Snap.' She smiled at him and saw
the suppressed humour in his eyes. She turned to Sophie.
'What's first?'

Sophie handed her a file and, taking a deep breath,
turned and picked up the phone. 'It's been ringing constantly since the accident. Hello…' She gave her name
and listened intently to the caller. Nicolette shrugged and
headed into EC-3, which was where her first patient was
waiting for her.

It was another three hours before things started to settle
down again.

'Ready to go?' Stephen asked Nicolette as she walked
across to the nurses' station.

'Yes, if we're allowed out of here, that is.'

'Go.' Stephanie was sitting at the nurses' station, talking to her brother. 'Things are under control here…sort
of.' She smiled tiredly at them. 'If we need you back, I'll
call, but for now, with the urgent cases being airlifted to
Sydney and the majority of patients seen to, we're able
to cope with what we have left.'

Nicolette glanced up at the clock. 'Is that the time?'
She checked her watch.

Stephanie smiled. 'I've heard it flies when you're having fun.'

'Three o'clock? It's really three o'clock?'

'Time to at least get some sleep before you need to be at work later this morning.'

'Good point.' Nicolette quickly hugged Stephanie and headed for the door. She waited while Stephen also hugged his sister.

'It's your day off tomorrow so I'll expect you around for brunch. Eleven o'clock at the latest.'

Stephanie leaned her head on his shoulder for a second and then looked up at him. 'I'll see you then.'

Stephen kissed her forehead. 'You be safe.'

'I will. Now go before something else happens.'

Nicolette yawned as they walked to the car. Stephen opened her door and seated her before heading around to the driver's side. 'I can't believe how tired I feel. It's like I looked at the clock and all of a sudden I'm tired.'

'Your body is being allowed to relax,' Stephen commented as he pulled out of the hospital grounds. 'Yawning is a common reaction.'

Nicolette yawned again and laughed as she raised her hand to cover her mouth. 'Common is right. Now I can't stop.'

'I'll drop you at home and then bring your car around.'

'I'm fine, Stephen.'

'You're in no state to drive—even the short distance between our houses. You get yourself to bed and I'll leave your keys in an envelope in the letterbox.'

'It's OK.' She tried again.

'Nicolette. I'm trying to be chivalrous. Don't destroy it.'

'Oh.' She smiled and closed her eyes, leaning thankfully back against the headrest. 'In that case, go ahead and be my knight in shining armour. I only hope you manage to stick around a bit longer than the others.'

'Others?'

'The ones whose armour turned out to be extremely tarnished, especially when they didn't get their own way.' She was babbling, she knew, but she didn't seem able to stop herself.

'Your boyfriends?' Stephen said the words so quietly that for a moment she thought she'd imagined it.

'*Past* boyfriends,' she stressed. 'I don't know. I just seem so unlucky in love.'

'You're not the only one.'

'Really?' She opened her eyes and glanced at him. 'How many women have you dated since Simone?'

Stephen shuddered at the other woman's name. 'None. She was scary enough for me.'

'What went so wrong? Apart from her being the clinging type, I mean.'

'Isn't that enough?' He laughed without humour. 'My mother was dying, as I've told you, and Simone was jealous of my spare time—not that I had much.'

'You said she didn't know about your mother.'

'She didn't know my mother was sick. Simone knew I was visiting my mother and she couldn't stand it. She even followed me a few times to make sure I wasn't cheating on her, but she never understood the relationship I had with my mother so what hope would she have had understanding the one I have with Steph? Simone is a woman who has a lot to give to a needy man. I am not a needy man. If she'd known my mother was dying, she probably would have wanted to meet her. She may have even offered to nurse her and, quite frankly, I loved my mother too much to put her through that. Simone would have smothered us both.'

'So you broke it off.'

'I tried to end it but she wouldn't accept it.'

That fitted with what Nicolette knew. Simone had tried her hardest to make it work and had then been offended when Stephen hadn't. At least, that's what Nicolette had been told.

'How long after your mother's death did you leave London?'

'Once all the paperwork had been completed. I was working on a research project at the time. It directly related to my mother's condition and she agreed to be a test subject. Needless to say, the treatment didn't work.'

'Didn't work at all?' Nicolette was surprised. From what she knew of Stephen, he wasn't the type of man to make incorrect calculations.

'It gave her an extra few months but—'

'There you go, then.'

'But there's no concrete proof the treatment was successful. It could have just been Mum hanging on until we could get Stephanie over to London so she could say goodbye.'

'You were both with her?'

'Yes.'

'I'm glad.'

'So were we.'

'And then you enlisted with the medical aid organisation. I'll bet Stephanie wasn't too happy.'

'Er…no, but finally she realised it was something I needed to do.'

'She said you got shot.'

'It was a flesh wound.' He brushed her words away. They were driving past the accident site they'd attended earlier, and although most of the debris had been cleared away there were still crews working, hoping to have everything done before the morning traffic began.

'I wonder what time those guys will end up quitting,' Nicolette mumbled as Stephen carefully navigated the area.

'What time do you start clinic?'

'Eight-thirty, and it will probably be hectic. It usually is after a major incident. If people were involved but weren't seriously injured, they'll leave it until morning before seeking medical attention. Then there are the people who just want to come in and gossip and find out exactly what happened.'

'Sounds like fun,' he said drolly.

'Oh, yeah. Much more fun than having brunch with your sister.'

Stephen nodded. 'I'll bet.' He turned off onto the main road of Blackheath, the early morning fog wrapping itself around them as he drove towards Nicolette's house.

'Honestly, Stephen, I'll be fine to drive home.'

'Chivalry. Remember?'

She held up her hands in surrender. 'Fine.'

'Besides, I can sleep in and you can't so the sooner you're tucked up in bed the better.'

'I don't think knights in shining armour are allowed to rub it in like that.'

'Really?'

'I'm pretty sure they're not. I'll have to check the rule book.'

'There are rules to being a knight in shining armour?' He pulled up outside her house.

'There are with me.'

'Mind if I have a copy? I wouldn't want to make any mistakes.'

Nicolette undid her seat belt and shifted to face him. 'Really? Why?'

Stephen hesitated for a second and she wished there was more light so she could see his face more clearly, but there wasn't. Still, the atmosphere between them for that one second intensified and she wondered whether he was going to kiss her goodnight. She certainly hoped so because since he'd pressed his lips to hers on the night of the fire, she'd been longing, almost desperately, for him to do it again, regardless of how many lectures she had given herself on the topic.

'Why?' The repeated word was whispered from him and he reached out a hand and tucked a stray strand of blonde hair behind her ear. 'Because I need to know where the boundaries are.'

Nicolette couldn't move. Her heart was pounding furiously against her chest and blood was pumping wildly in her ears. He was going to kiss her again. Joy! Her tongue slid out to wet her lips in anticipation and she leaned in a little closer, her breathing so loud she was positive he could hear it. The windows in the car were starting to steam up, even though the heater and demister were on.

His hand caressed her cheek and her eyelids fluttered closed for an instant. She was going to be his undoing, he realised, and although he wanted nothing more than to lean over and press his lips to hers, as he'd been dying to do for weeks now, he knew he shouldn't. Not when they would start working together next week.

'You are so beautiful.' His deep voice washed over her and she gasped as his thumb brushed across her parted lips. 'But we can't.'

His words took a few seconds to penetrate the haze surrounding her mind. 'Stephen?'

He swallowed and, after exhaling harshly, dropped his hand and pulled back. 'Nicolette…I care about you, you must realise that.'

'And I care about you.'

'But we've both been hurt in the past and come Monday…' He trailed off.

'Come Monday we'll be working together,' she finished for him, her eyes stinging with tears. She cleared her throat, trying to get control over her voice. 'I know.'

'Believe me, I want nothing more than to kiss you right now.'

The butterflies that had been lying dormant in her stomach began twirling with excitement at his words. 'That's what I want, too,' she assured him eagerly.

'But we can't.'

'Not even one last time?' She sounded desperate yet she couldn't let him go, not just yet.

'It wouldn't change anything.'

'No. That's true but it would make us both feel better.'

'It's only a temporary bandage, though. We can't begin a relationship when we'll be working together. It's too risky. If something were to go wrong between us, it would make our working lives intolerable. We've both been there before, we've both experienced what it's like to work with someone you've been involved with, and I can't just walk away from my practice so that would mean you would be the one leaving and that's not fair. Not to you, not to me.'

She knew what he spoke was the truth and the fact he was trying to protect them both only endeared him to her even more. *What if it did work out?* She was too scared to voice the thought. It was too risky. Right now, though, she didn't want to deal with truths. She wanted to deal with fantasy. 'Tonight.' She reached out and touched his cheek. The palm of her hand and her fingertips tingled from the stubble there. Those tingles made their way up her arm before zinging their way through her entire body. The explosion, from a mere touch, was enough to give her courage to say what she wanted to say. 'Tonight,' she repeated, 'you're my knight in shining armour. You've rescued me from endless patients…' She ran her fingers through his hair and he sucked in a breath. 'You've driven me home through fog-infested streets…' She cupped his cheek and he angled his face into her hand. 'And it's protocol that you kiss me.' She brushed her thumb across his lips and he groaned, his gaze never leaving hers. At least she was able to evoke as much of a reaction in him as he had been able to do in her.

'Protocol,' he murmured, his breathing becoming more insane as the moments ticked on. What could it hurt? They both knew the score. They both knew what was at stake and, as she had said, it would be a goodbye kiss, effectively ending it before it began. 'I'm a man who always follows protocol,' he said finally, and she almost sighed with relief.

He was going to capitulate. He was going to give them both what they wanted, what they needed, because after this kiss, there would be nothing…only drought. As though in slow motion he switched off the engine with one hand and released his seat belt with the other.

'You know I've been fighting the urge to do this for what seems like for ever,' he said softly into the sudden stillness.

'I know. I've been fighting, too, but after what we've just been through I'm not feeling very strong right now. I need your comfort, I need your touch… I need you, Stephen, at least one last time.'

It was what he wanted to hear. Both of them knew the

risks, both of them knew the score. It was a mutual good-bye kiss and afterwards they would be professional colleagues who enjoyed the same sense of humour. That was all.

He reached out to release her gorgeous blonde locks from the clip. Her hair tumbled down instantly, cascading around her shoulders. With almost trembling fingers he plunged them into the silky softness and groaned, urging her head closer, leaning his body towards her.

'You're incredible.' He pressed his lips to hers in a firm kiss, holding them in limbo for a few seconds before pulling back to gaze into her eyes.

Her lips parted as she gasped, not caring in the least that he'd left her panting with anticipation. Once more she brushed her thumb across his lips but this time his tongue flicked out to wet it before drawing it into his mouth, suckling it.

He watched as her dazed eyes opened wider. Did the woman have any idea just how much she was affecting him? He was beginning to burn, he was igniting and fanning the flames. The question he didn't know the answer to was, would he ever be able to put it out? It only fuelled his impatience and quickly he released her thumb, wanting to have his mouth on hers once more.

When they finally came together, their mouths were open, ready and seeking each other. Where the kiss outside the burning house had been gentle and testing, this one was wild and passionate, taking them both to extraordinary heights such as neither had ever felt before.

His hands were fisted in her hair, holding her head in place. She wasn't going anywhere—he wouldn't let her. The possessiveness he'd felt earlier towards her began to intensify and he realised even though this was a goodbye kiss, at least he'd still be able to see her, to spend time with her without the hassles of a physical relationship. At the moment, though, he realised a physical relationship with Nicolette wouldn't be a hassle at all!

Her hands were at the back of his neck, kneading urgently against his muscles. It was mildly relaxing yet powerful at the same time, and the only thought that kept reverberating around his mind was how badly he needed her…more so with each passing second their lips remained locked together.

Hungrily, they took from each other, knowing this moment needed to last them for ever if they were going to make their professional relationship work. After this there was no going back, and because of that neither was in a hurry to break the embrace.

It was just the two of them. Nothing existed beyond this moment and she found herself wishing for a way to make time stand still. How could she have ever thought she could just be this man's friend? A friend didn't create such havoc with her senses. A friend didn't take her up so high she could see the world spread out before her. A friend didn't turn everything she'd ever known on its head, but that was exactly what he was doing and she was loving every minute of it.

Loving?

The thought made her pull back and gaze into his face. His eyes snapped open in confusion, both of them breathing rapidly.

'What's wrong?'

Nicolette focused on those intense blue eyes—what she could see of them in the dark—and she knew. She knew her emotions were no longer at all platonic where Stephen was concerned. Her emotions were more, *much* more. In fact, they were everything.

Here, sitting in front of her, was the man she loved.

'What's wrong?' he repeated. 'Did I hurt you?' He loosened his grip on her hair, his fingers now gently sifting through her locks in a caress. The action created a relaxing pressure on her scalp but it was his caring, his thoughtfulness and his downright gorgeousness that caused the goose bumps to break out over her skin.

'I'm fine.' How was she supposed to tell him? Should she tell him? And if so, what then? 'I just needed oxygen.'

Stephen smiled, the first real smile without inhibitions, without force and without teasing. It was mind-blowing and she was positive her heart skipped a beat. 'I guess we got a little carried away.'

'A little?' She raised an eyebrow, desperate to cover over her real emotions but at the same time wanting to blurt them out to the whole world. She loved Stephen Brooks. *She loved Stephen Brooks!* 'I'd better get inside.'

'Already?' The word was out before he could stop it.

'Stephen.' She pressed her mouth briefly to his simply because she couldn't resist the worried little schoolboy look which had just crossed his face. 'We can't stay here, making out in the car for the rest of the morning.' For some reason the knowledge that she loved him had given her extra strength to step away from him, whereas before the kiss, before she'd realised the depth of her true feelings, she'd been clinging to him like a koala. 'Besides, I have clinic, remember.'

Stephen frowned, his smile vanishing into thin air. 'I remember.' His tone was a little gruff yet the touch of his fingers in her hair was still sweet and gentle. 'We need to get you to bed.'

She couldn't help the gasp that escaped at the words and she could feel herself blushing, thankful for the darkness around them. 'Yes.'

Without warning he pressed his mouth to hers once

more and both were instantly catapulted back to where they'd been only moments before. This time, though, it wasn't as hot and hungry as it had been. His mouth moved over hers with a calm satisfaction and a growing sense of familiarity.

The intensity was still there. The desperation was still there and the love she felt for him was still there.

On and on his gentle onslaught went, and this time, instead of her fingers kneading the back of his neck, her hands travelled slowly down, coming to rest on his chest. He could feel his heart pounding and knew she could feel it, too. He didn't care. He wanted her to know how she affected him, how important she'd become and how he couldn't possibly risk a relationship with her. She was too delicious, too enigmatic and far too incredible for her own good. He didn't want to hurt her and he wouldn't.

'*Tu es sexy,*' he murmured as he broke the kiss, planting small butterfly kisses on her cheeks.

'*Et toi aussi.*'

'*Tu es belle et intellegente.*' More butterfly kisses on her neck as he worked his way around to her ear.

She smiled, her eyes closed as she enjoyed the sensations he was evoking. '*Merci.*' Then she gasped and jerked back so she could look at him. 'You speak French?'

'*Oui, mademoiselle.*' He nuzzled her, wanting to kiss his way to her other ear.

Nicolette thought of the few times she'd mumbled in French and all this time he'd understood her. Embarrassment touched her briefly but she shrugged it off. That was the least of her worries. Her first and foremost priority—apart from enjoying his kisses way too much—was the fact that she was in love with him! '*Ça me plaît.*'

'I'm glad you like it.' His deep voice washed over her.

'Pas toi?'

'Me? Of course I like it. I like feeling you beneath my lips, I like feeling the way you respond to me.'

'Then why are we saying goodbye?' she urged.

Stephen lifted his head and exhaled sadly. 'Because we have to, you know that. We discussed it.'

'Yes, but that was before—' She stopped. If she told him right now she loved him, she'd probably scare him away. It was clear he didn't feel the same way about her otherwise he wouldn't be saying what he was saying. She needed time. Time to think. Time to sort herself out. And she could only do that when she wasn't within kissing distance of him.

'Before,' she continued, 'I realised you were going to make this the most incredible goodbye kiss I've ever experienced. It was so…' She searched desperately for the right word.

He nodded. 'I know. It was, wasn't it?'

'See? So why can't we give it a go?'

'Give what a go exactly?'

'I don't know. Dating.'

'It won't work.'

'How do you know?'

'Because I know me.'

'Does this have anything to do with Simone?'

'No, and neither does it have anything to do with any of your ex-boyfriends. I'm just not ready. I haven't been in the Blue Mountains long and my dream of getting my own practice up and running is finally coming true. I want to enjoy that for a while. I want to spend time with Stephanie and also time alone. I'm sorry if that sounds selfish, but that's just where I am. Dating doesn't fit into the scenario and I know for a fact that I'd only end up hurting you.'

His words made sense. He'd not long returned from a war zone and she knew at first-hand how it could take a while to sort yourself out after such a mind-altering experience. She'd only done six months, Stephen had done twelve. Although she'd had a gun held to her head, she'd never actually been shot. Stephen had.

'You *need* to be selfish.' She nodded with understanding.

'Don't say it like that.'

'I'm not being mean, Stephen, I'm being factual, and I completely agree with you. I was the same when I got back from my time in North Africa. You need to process everything, find out where your old life—before the war zone—and new life meet.'

Stephen was astounded. He frowned and then shook his head in amazement. 'You really do understand.'

'Yes, and I think it's great you realise this, otherwise you'd probably end up having a breakdown in a few more months.'

'So you're willing to be friends?'

'Of course.'

He waited. 'But?' he prompted.

'No buts.' She smiled at him and leaned back to get her bag from the back seat. 'Hey, and don't worry about doing the car shuffle now. It's almost four o'clock and you need to rest as well. I'll walk around in the morning and get the car. Hopefully, the brisk walk will wake me up.' She smiled, hoping to lighten the atmosphere.

Nicolette put her hand on the door lever and leaned over, brushing a feather-light kiss across his lips. 'Thank you.' With that, she pushed open the door, climbed from the car and walked towards the house. The sensor light, which flicked on, momentarily blinded her as she fished out her keys. Stephen's car hadn't moved and she knew he was waiting to see her safely inside—that's what knights in shining armour did.

Once she had the front door open she turned and waved, before heading inside and closing it behind her. She leaned against it, listening as he started the car again and slowly drove away into the foggy night.

Nicolette breathed deeply. She was in love with Stephen, and Stephen needed time. Time she could do. Denying the attraction—that would have been harder to fight, but tonight both of them had openly admitted the attraction so she didn't have to worry about that.

Time. She would give him time and she would also give him the help she knew he needed. She'd had her brother Luc to help her navigate the minefield of emotions she'd experienced in Africa. You were always so busy you hardly had time to deal with them, but back in your own world it was a whole new ball game and sometimes emotions would spring up out of nowhere and assail you.

Yes, she decided firmly. Stephen would need help navigating his emotional minefield and she was the perfect person to help him. After all, she loved him.

CHAPTER NINE

NICOLETTE walked out into the waiting room, calling her last patient for Friday morning through to her consulting room.

'Mrs Bevan. You're looking well. How's your cat Clayton?'

'Oh, he's fine, Doctor. I say, this is a very pretty place, isn't it?' Mrs Bevan pointed around the room to the tasteful artwork Stephen had hung on the walls. 'I remember this house from many years ago, and I can honestly say it's never looked so good.'

'I'll certainly pass that on to Dr Brooks.'

'He supervised the transformation, did he? I suppose he would as he owns the place.'

'No, Dr Brooks *did* the transformation. He sanded and painted and fixed and hammered. The first time I came here, there were ladders and paint tins and everything everywhere.'

'He did it himself?' Mrs Bevan was impressed. 'And how long have you been working here?'

'Since the practice opened at the beginning of last week.'

'Has it been busy?'

'Very, but that's the way it's supposed to be. So you're here for your check-up?'

'Yes.'

'Dr Brooks is interested in looking at the scans you had done.' Nicolette glanced around. 'You did bring them with you, didn't you?'

'I gave them to that lovely receptionist.'

'Not to worry.' Nicolette picked up the phone and spoke to the receptionist. 'First of all, let me have a listen to your chest, and once I've done your general check-up we'll call Dr Brooks in.'

Nicolette listened to her patient's chest and declared herself well satisfied. She continued with the examination and when she was finished she called through to Stephen's consulting room, which was just down the hallway.

The time they'd been working together had been the happiest of her life. She was in love and for the first time ever she wasn't psychoanalysing it. She was just enjoying it, and seeing Stephen almost every day certainly helped.

After their earth-shattering goodbye kiss, Nicolette had spent a few days mulling over her new emotions for him and she'd had a revelation. In all her past relationships they'd never really been friends. Oh, sure, there had been mutual attraction and they'd enjoyed doing things together, but close friends? No. The relationships had been strictly girlfriend and boyfriend, not friendship *and* relationship, and she'd realised with a pang that that was exactly what she wanted with Stephen.

At first they'd both been careful not to be alone together, not to be caught in the kitchen making coffee at the same time, not to be sitting down eating lunch together, but it had only lasted a few days. Once the initial awkwardness had passed, they regularly found themselves eating together. Sometimes their receptionist joined them. Either way, Nicolette was getting to know Stephen a lot better.

She was becoming more in tune with his wry humour and even when he smiled at her, instead of freaking out about the way he made her feel, she simply accepted it and enjoyed it.

There was a brisk knock at her door before he came in. 'Mrs Bevan. How nice to see you again. How's Clayton? Behaving himself, I hope.'

'Oh, yes, Dr Brooks.' The woman giggled and Nicolette loved Stephen all the more simply for the way he cared for others.

Stephen held up the radiology packet. 'I gather these are yours so why don't we all look at them together?' He flicked on the viewing box and pulled out the first scan. 'Looking good.' They looked at a few more before he declared himself satisfied. 'I'd like you to see us both at least once a week until your cardiologist's appointment— which is in a few weeks, I believe?' He glanced at Nicolette for confirmation.

'Three weeks' time,' Nicolette confirmed.

'Great. Until then, stay warm, stay out of the cool night air and, most of all, keep Clayton under control.'

Again, Mrs Bevan giggled like a schoolgirl. 'Yes, Dr Brooks.' After he'd left, she sighed. 'He's so lovely,' she told Nicolette.

'Yes, he is.' Nicolette tapped on the keyboard and set a form into the printer. 'Here's a new prescription for you and make sure you call the surgery or the hospital if you have any pain or just don't feel well.' Her words were firm yet kind.

'Yes, dear.'

'Don't feel as though you're bothering us because we love to be bothered, especially Dr Brooks.'

Mrs Bevan smiled again at the mention of Stephen. 'All right, dear. Thank you.'

Once Nicolette had finished inputting Mrs Bevan's notes, she headed thankfully into the kitchen, eager for lunch. She found Stephen there, sitting at the table, munching on a sandwich.

'What are you eating?'

'Peanut butter and jam.'

'Really? I craved them the whole time I was in Africa. Tea?'

'Thanks.' Stephen frowned.

'What's wrong?' Nicolette took two cups out and popped tea bags into them.

'I craved them the whole time I was there, too.'

Nicolette laughed. 'We only had jam.'

'We only had peanut butter,' he said, and joined in her laughter.

'If only we could have got your peanut butter together with my jam, we both would have been satisfied.' As she placed his cup of tea on the table in front of him, their gazes met and held. Quickly, she turned away and opened the fridge, pulling out the ingredients she would need. 'Would you like another one? The best way to eat them is when they're freshly made.'

He cleared his throat. 'Sure.' When she'd finished and was sitting down, Stephen placed his hand over hers. Nicolette flinched a little but only because he'd surprised her with the contact. Warmth spread up her arm and burst through the rest of her, and she welcomed every last second of the feeling. She glanced up and met his gaze once more. 'Thanks,' he murmured, his tone intense, his voice husky.

'You're welcome.' Her words were genuine and heartfelt, which caused Stephen to raise a questioning eyebrow.

'Do you know what I'm thanking you for?' He removed his hand from hers and raked it through his hair, a little unsteady at the thought that she knew him so well.

'For being your friend.' Nicolette took a bite of her sandwich. 'Mmm. Yummy.' She swallowed her mouthful and smiled at him. 'And even though you didn't say thank you for the tea or the sandwich, I'll let you off, but only this once.'

'Thank you,' he said again, this time in a more normal tone. 'I'm constantly surprised at how well you seem to know me.'

She smiled. 'It's natural. We've had a lot of similar experiences.'

He thought about that, then slowly nodded. 'Just talking to you the past few weeks about little things such as this…' He gestured to the sandwich. 'It's made a big difference.'

'I'm glad. It's hard to kind of shift your past experiences into your new world. It's as though you've had your blinkers taken off when you see such tragedy and devastation and although we saw that three weeks ago with that horrific accident, it's not something that happens every single day—thank God. When you return to your normal life, it's hard to try and match the two worlds up.'

'Yes,' he replied enthusiastically. 'That's exactly it.'

'It took me quite a few months but I had my brother helping me. He's had similar experiences.'

Again Stephen processed her words and then gave another slow nod. 'And you've been helping me, even though I didn't know it.'

For a moment, she wasn't sure whether he was happy about it or whether he resented it. 'Who else do you have contact with who understands what you've been through?' she asked. 'Sure you have Stephanie but—'

'Steph has her own problems at the moment.'

Nicolette was concerned. 'She's all right, isn't she? Not doing anything silly?'

The little grin she was becoming accustomed to touched his lips. 'She's fine, healthwise. Extremely frustrated and very interested in the new A and E director.'

'Oliver? She never said. We had coffee yesterday and she never breathed a word.'

'She's still fighting her feelings.'

'Does that mean you get them?'

He laughed. 'I hope not. Anyway, I invited her around for brunch on Sunday but she can't make it. She's helping Oliver with his daughter.'

'Sounds…intriguing.' Nicolette smiled. 'Wait a minute. Aren't they sharing a house?'

'That's right.'

'I'm still not sure how that happened.'

'You know a friend of ours lent her his house?'

'Yes.'

'Well, at the same time the estate agent leased it to Oliver.'

'So why didn't she move back in with you?'

He hesitated a moment. 'She didn't want to cramp my style.'

'As if she'd do that. She's your sis—' Nicolette stopped, belatedly grasping Stephen's meaning. 'Oh. *That* kind of style.'

'Exactly.'

Nicolette thought back to the conversations she'd had with Stephanie about Stephen. 'You did tell her we're just friends, didn't you?'

'Didn't *you*?' he countered with a curious grin.

'Yes, I did.' Nicolette shrugged. 'Not that she believed me.'

'Or me.'

'So now she's getting interested in Oliver. Well, well.' She sipped her tea. 'What do you think of him? I'm sure your opinion would matter a lot to her.'

'It does, which is scary.'

'Doesn't her opinion matter to you?'

'Yes.' Stephen shifted in his seat, a little uncomfortable at the thought. When he'd told Stephanie that he was only going to be friends with Nicolette, his sister had laughed. She'd kissed his cheek and given him her blessing, telling him she could think of no one who was as perfect for him as Nicolette was. She'd also said if he needed to keep fooling himself for a bit longer, that was fine but not to leave it too long.

In all honesty, Stephen had thought working with Nicolette might cause more problems than he'd anticipated, especially after their goodbye kiss. His body had craved her, his hands itched to feel the silky softness of her hair, his mouth eager to have a repeat performance. His mind, however, had been well satisfied because much to his surprise they'd been not only working well together but also having amazing discussions.

At first he'd thought it might be a little strained or tense but she'd breezed in, treated him almost like a brother and given everything to her work. He was glad to know they could just be colleagues and friends. It was rare and he'd never felt as comfortable with another woman as he did with Nicolette—except perhaps with Stephanie, but she was his twin.

'Earth to Stephen?' Nicolette waved her hand in front of his face. 'You all right?'

He blinked and realised he'd been staring off into space. 'Yes. Sorry,' he replied briskly. He turned his attention to the rest of his lunch and began to eat.

'So?' Nicolette said after a few mouthfuls. 'What do you think of him?'

'Who?'

She laughed. 'Well, that says it all. Oliver.'

'I've worked a few shifts with him and he seems OK

but I'm not one to rush judgements. Steph, on the other hand, is jumping in with both feet.'

'That concerns you?'

'When *doesn't* Steph concern me.' He smiled. 'She seems crazy about his daughter so I suppose that's a bonus.'

Nicolette thought for a moment before saying, 'Oliver seems very grounded…more serious I mean…almost the complete opposite to Stephanie.'

'Ever heard that opposites attract?'

'Does that mean he's going to dye his hair red?'

'Red is the opposite of green?' Stephen swallowed his last bite and stood.

'Of course it is, unless Stephanie dyes her hair some other colour.'

'Which is always on the cards. She also mentioned something about going to Sydney on Sunday.'

'I thought she was helping Oliver on Sunday?'

'She's helping him in Sydney.'

'Interesting.'

'Which brings me back to my point. As Steph can't make it for brunch, would you like to come around? I've already bought everything,' he added by way of explanation.

The food in Nicolette's mouth turned to sawdust but she managed to swallow it before having a sip of her tea. 'Are you…?' She stopped and cleared her throat. 'Are you sure that's a good idea?'

'The two of us alone, you mean?'

'Yes.'

'We agreed to be friends and that's what we are.'

As much as Nicolette desperately wanted to say yes, she knew the answer had to be no. Although she loved being with him at the clinic and getting to know him better, to go around to his house without the protection of getting interrupted either by patients, the receptionist or emergencies was far too risky.

'I don't think so, Stephen, but thanks for the invite.'

He frowned. 'It would just be two colleagues eating food. Nothing more.'

Nicolette stood and carried her plate and cup to the sink. 'I still think it's too risky.'

'Why?' he urged. 'We can continue the discussion we had the other day on the new vaccine that's out or swap more war stories.'

'And tell me, Stephen, what do we do when *this* happens?' Nicolette took a step closer, directly into his personal space. Standing almost toe to toe, she was instantly aware of the warmth radiating from his body. His hypnotic scent wove its way about her senses, making her sigh with longing.

Her gaze slowly travelled up from the knot of his tie, taking in the mildly angular jaw which already held a hint of his approaching five-o'clock shadow. His lips came into view and she felt a surge of wonderment flood through her as she remembered how incredible it had been to feel his mouth on hers, seeking and demanding an equal response. His nose, which had a slight bump in it, indicating a break long ago, and then those amazing blue eyes which never failed to elicit a response from deep within her.

'What would you do if I kissed you right now?' she whispered. He was so close she could almost taste him. He opened his mouth to speak but closed it quickly and cleared his throat.

'Hmm?' She knew if one single part of their bodies touched, both would be unable to control the power they would unleash. She glanced up from his mouth to look into his eyes, seeing the answer before her. If she kissed him right now, there was no way he'd be able to resist— and that was her point.

He carefully cleared his throat, his gaze moving from her lips and back to her eyes before he spoke. 'We don't let it happen.' He didn't try and move away, which indicated he was enjoying the torture as much as she was.

'My point exactly.' Although it almost killed her, she finally moved, putting distance between them. Both had to wait for a few moments for their breathing to return to normal.

Stephen shook his head and raked an unsteady hand through his hair. 'It's so…'

'I know,' she said quickly, proving once more that they were on the same wavelength. 'Stephen, working together is great and, yes, we've come to know each other better during the past few weeks and professionally I am very happy working here. It's great but if we're going to succeed in suppressing the attraction between us we can't put ourselves in positions where it's impossible not to follow through,' she urged. 'Having brunch with you… I want nothing more than to say yes but I also know we'd end up breaking the bond we've formed and that could cause more problems.'

'I agree.'

Nicolette sighed with frustration. 'I was sure you would. Now, if you'll excuse me, I have a few errands to run before afternoon clinic begins.'

'Of course.' As she started out of the room he called her name. 'Sorry. I forgot to ask when you're next rostered on at the hospital.'

'Tomorrow night.'

'So am I. I'll get someone in to cover the practice.'

She raised an eyebrow. 'Stephanie playing matchmaker again?'

'Oliver's doing the rosters now. She forced him to.'

'Oh, yes. Of course.' She felt a little embarrassed at her words. 'All right, I'd better go. Ah...is there anything you need? Letters posted? Stationery?'

'No. No. I'm fine, thanks.'

With a quick nod she disappeared around the corner. Stephen turned his attention to washing the dishes before heading into his consulting room. He paced up and down. What on earth was he supposed to do? For the past few weeks, he'd found it increasingly difficult to get Nicolette out of his mind, especially working so closely with her. He was aching for her but he knew if he gave in, he could ruin everything.

This wasn't the first time he'd been stuck between a rock and a hard place, and in the past he'd always made the right decision. He had to rely on those gut instincts to see him through this time and although Nicolette was stirring his blood almost to boiling point each time she smiled at him, he needed to remain firm in his decision. Getting involved would only cause more problems because in the end it would be Nicolette who would need to leave the practice and possibly the area when things went wrong.

But what if they *don't* go wrong? a small voice inside his heart asked. What if he followed through on his passion and desire for Nicolette and they both lived happily ever after?

'No.' He spoke the word out loud as he walked around his desk and sat in his chair. It wouldn't work.

Why not? asked the voice. During the past few weeks they'd both shown they had more in common than just work. They had the same sense of humour, liked similar music, had enjoyed rousing political debates. He loved how, right after her last patient left, she'd tear the clips from her hair and shake her head, often running her fingers through her hair, gently massaging her scalp. At first he'd thought she'd just been doing it to drive him crazy but day after day she went through the same routine, sometimes when he was in the room, but at other times she'd walk out with her bag in one hand and her hairclips in the other, the gorgeous blonde locks falling tantalisingly around her shoulders.

Stephen massaged his temples, knowing he needed to figure this out—and soon, or it would tear them apart. His phone rang and he instantly snatched it up. 'Hi, Steph.'

'Hi yourself. Having fun?'

'Not really.'

'I thought as much. This is just a quick call because I'm about to walk out the door and head to work. So what's going on? More angst over Nic?'

'I doubt it will ever go away,' he mumbled.

'It'll only go away if you face it. Have you told her how you feel?'

'The attraction is mutual, Steph.'

'It's amazing that you can be more stubborn than me. I'm not talking about the attraction. Do you love her?'

He opened his mouth to reply but stopped. It was on the tip of his tongue to say he didn't really know her that well but realised it was a lie. He *did* know her, and what he knew he certainly liked. 'I don't know.'

'Well...' she drawled. 'That's an improvement on "I hardly know her", which is what you've said in the past. So she's still succeeding in driving you crazy, eh? Way to go, Nic.'

'Steph, this is hardly helping.'

'Look. There's another reason why I called. Oliver has

a friend coming to town tomorrow morning and we thought it would be nice to introduce him to Nicolette.'

'Why?' The word came out between clenched teeth and he felt as though his intestines had just been tied in several knots. No! He wanted to yell the word at his sister, to let her know Nicolette was not available, that she already had plans—even though he wasn't sure one way or the other whether that was true.

'Because she's a nice person, she's single and this guy sounds like her type.'

'I'm a nice person, I'm single and how on earth would you know what her type is?' he growled fiercely, his gut churning.

'I'm her friend. Girls talk.' Stephanie began to giggle and then he caught on.

'You're playing me.' It was a statement and he shook his head, unable to believe he'd fallen for the oldest trick in the book—the jealousy trick.

'So how did you feel, eh? Does the thought of Nicolette with any other man make you crazy? Personally, I think the answer is yes,' she went on before he could say a word.

'Well, if you want to talk about romance, Steph, let me give you a little quiz about Oliver.'

'Oh, gee. Is that the time? I have to go now, bro.' She laughed. 'See you later. Love you.' She hung up and he was left holding the receiver.

Stephen shook his head, annoyed that Steph had been right. His gut was still churning with the thought of Nicolette smiling at another man, being drawn into his arms, being kissed by him. He slammed the receiver into the cradle and started pacing the room.

Nicolette with another man? Never!

There was no way in the world he could let that happen.

and the thought terrified him. The woman had come into his life and promptly turned it completely inside out and upside down, and it was the last thing he needed. She said she understood about him trying to sort his mind out yet when she looked at him with those big brown eyes, he felt as though he could drown in them. The feel of her hair, the touch of her lips against his, her body firmly pressed to his own. These were the things that mattered.

In all fairness to her it wasn't her fault she was so irresistible and he could tell she was really trying to make his friendship thing between them work, but when she'd stepped so close to him to prove her point, his heart had started hammering wildly against his chest, the need, the urge for her to be his and his alone overpowering.

She belonged to him.

The urgency of his feelings surprised him. They were archaic, caveman-like yet the possessiveness he felt towards Nicolette remained strong and true. The only thing he needed to figure out now was, what was he going to do about it?

CHAPTER TEN

'MY FEET are killing me.' Lauren sat down to write up some notes. Although Nicolette had worked with the pretty brunette several times, they'd never really connected. 'What a hectic night.'

'You can say that again,' Nicolette murmured as she finished writing her own set of notes. Although they'd been busy, it hadn't been traumatic.

'People always leave it until night-time when the temperature drops to below zero before they realise they're sick.'

Nicolette smiled. 'People don't want to think about their symptoms when it's nice and warm outside, and we did actually have some sunshine this morning, which was a miracle in itself.' She glanced up, a movement catching her eye. Stephen was coming out of an examination cubicle with a patient, talking earnestly to them. Her heart turned over with love at the sight of him. They'd been working together all night and although they'd hardly spoken a word, it was still nice to know he was around.

Lauren looked up, too. 'Mmm. Dr Dishy. What's it like seeing him every day at his consulting rooms?'

'No different from any other doctor,' Nicolette blatantly lied. She forced herself to look away, trying to remember what on earth she was supposed to be doing. Thankfully her shift was almost over as she couldn't deal with other women drooling over the man she was in love with...*really* in love with, not just infatuated as Lauren was.

'Anyone else come in?' Stephen asked, and Nicolette almost jumped out of her skin. She hadn't realised he'd come to the nurses' station.

'No. We're pretty settled for the moment, Stephen,' Lauren replied, fluttering her eyelashes and giving him a coy little smile. 'Sit down for a moment and relax.'

He nodded politely and did as she'd suggested, flicking open the casenotes and filling them out. 'So…how's your practice going?' the nurse flirted.

Nicolette watched as Lauren stood and walked over to stand beside him, leaning back against the desk in a mildly provocative pose. 'You know, if you needed a nurse for the practice, I'd be more than happy to…fill any vacant position. I'm trained in immunisations and family medicine and I only do a couple of shifts here so apart from that I'm quite…free.'

'Thank you, Lauren.' Stephen glanced briefly at the nurse, giving her a small nod. 'I'll keep that in mind should I ever require a nurse.'

Nicolette groaned and stood, unable to watch or listen. Stephen spun around to look at her.

'You all right, Nicolette?'

She forced a smile even though inside she felt like dying. 'Fine.' The word came out in a higher pitch than she'd intended. Clearing her throat, she glanced down at her hands. 'I'm just going to get my bag. I'll be back to sign out,' she told Lauren, leaving the young nurse to do her best where Stephen was concerned. She had to remind herself that he was allowed to be interested in other women. They hadn't made a commitment to each other, which made them both free agents. If Stephen wanted to flirt with the nurses a little, who was she to comment? It was his business, not hers.

The words replayed over and over in her head as she

walked briskly to the female changing rooms, desperate to hold back the tears she could feel beginning to threaten. It's not your business, she kept mentally repeating. Her eyes began to fill, blurring her vision as she punched in the code. An error message beep sounded.

'Nicolette.'

She turned and could just make out Stephen walking towards her. No. Not now. She almost had herself under control. She tried the code again but couldn't see anything. Angrily she brushed the tears away, not wanting him to see her like that.

'Nicolette,' he called again, getting closer.

Two-six-oh-five. Her fingers finally pressed the keys in the right order and she pushed open the door, escaping inside. She stopped still for a second, breathing a sigh of relief. She was safe for the moment. He might be waiting when she came out but at least she had some time to get herself under control. She dug in her pocket for a tissue and dabbed at her eyes as she walked over to her locker. She blew her nose and, beginning to feel a little better, she squared her shoulders and took a deep breath. 'You can cope,' she told herself.

The buzz of the changing-room doors sounded but she didn't turn around. Instead, she pulled out her keys.

'Nicolette!' Stephen's voice startled her and she dropped them.

'What are you doing in here?' She rounded on him. 'Get out.'

'I want to talk to you, and I don't appreciate you ignoring me.'

'I'll be out in a moment.' She shooed him away with her hand. 'Go, before someone else comes in.'

He frowned at her. 'You're behaving rather strangely tonight. Has something happened?'

Only the fact that I'm so madly in love with you I can't cope with you talking to any other woman, she wanted to say. Instead, she shrugged. 'I'm tired. Do you have any complaints about my patient treatments?'

'No. That's not what I meant. You've been...distant somehow.'

Nicolette sighed and looked down at the tissue in her hands. She fidgeted with it for a moment longer before putting it in the bin. 'I'm fine, Stephen,' she reassured him.

He stepped closer and studied her face for a moment. 'You've been crying.'

'I'm fine.' She shifted back, keeping distance between them.

'So you keep telling me.' He thrust his hands into his trousers pockets. 'Look, we need to talk. Please, will you come over for brunch tomorrow?'

'Stephen.' Why was he torturing her like this? Didn't he get it? She could be the relaxed professional during clinic, she could work with him here at the hospital, she could even talk with him not only about their time spent in Africa but also about a variety of other topics. What she couldn't do was watch other women flirt with him or be alone in a room with him...like she was now. She loved him so passionately, so completely, so intensely it was getting harder with every passing second not to tell him the truth.

'I can't. You know that.'

He glanced down at the floor and then back at her, determination on his face. 'Actually, I want to discuss the practice with you. We haven't had a real practice meeting and this morning I realised there are several things we need to go over.'

Nicolette frowned, wondering if he was telling the truth

or whether this was just a ruse to get her there. If it was, why? He knew the score just as she did. Perhaps he thought, with the attraction the way it was between them, that he couldn't work with her after all. Panic began to grip her and she wanted to grab him and shake whatever it was out of him right now. He'd said he needed to discuss things so surely that didn't mean he was going to fire her. Admittedly the atmosphere yesterday afternoon hadn't been as relaxed as it had been before that moment in the kitchen at lunchtime.

'We can have the discussion now,' she suggested.

'In the female changing rooms? I don't think that's appropriate. Besides, we're both tired and the papers I need are at home. Tomorrow, around eleven?'

Nicolette swallowed over the tension gripping her and slowly nodded. 'Eleven, but not for brunch.'

Stephen thought for a moment before nodding. 'I'll see you then.' He turned and headed out of the changing rooms, stopping in the doorway. 'Drive safely tonight.'

'You, too.'

'Give me three rings when you get home so I know you're safe.'

Nicolette almost burst into tears at his thoughtfulness. Was it any wonder she loved him? 'You, too,' she insisted, smiling a little. He returned her smile and her heart melted into a pool of mush. With a brisk nod, he was gone.

He was so incredibly different from the others. Tim, Warren and Archie had all been men who'd put themselves first. It had been their careers that had mattered most in the relationships—not so with Stephen. They had appreciated her brains but had never really taken the time to have meaningful discussions with her—Stephen had. They had never made her feel as though she were the most valuable, precious and cherished woman in the whole entire world—Stephen definitely did.

He cared about her, that was evident, and he was certainly attracted to her, but could he possibly open his heart to let himself love her? She didn't know. She knew him better now than she had a few weeks ago, but was it enough? Dared she hope?

Nicolette retrieved her keys from the floor and opened her locker. She would see him tomorrow at eleven. He'd said he wanted to discuss the practice but why hadn't he said so before? Was it just a ruse, an excuse? Did he want to get her alone to let her know all contact and conversations, other than those of a professional nature, must stop? On the flipside, did he want to profess undying love?

She gripped her hands close to her heart and prayed fervently that that would be the case. She was a hopeless romantic, she realised as she opened her eyes, retrieved her coat, scarf and bag and closed her locker. Or maybe not hopeless but...hopeful.

When she signed out at the nurses' station, she noted Stephen had already left. The security guard walked her to her car and although it took a few attempts to get her car started, it took even longer for the heater to kick in. She needed to think seriously about getting a new car. Perhaps she could ask Stephen to come to Sydney with her when she was ready to buy one.

As promised, when she arrived home, she dialled his home number and let it ring. He picked up immediately. 'You weren't supposed to answer,' she protested. 'You were supposed to let it ring three times and then I was supposed to hang up.'

'Sorry. I just wanted to hear your voice and double-check you were all right.' His deep, caring voice washed over her and Nicolette slumped down into a chair. He really was everything she was looking for. She'd promised herself not to get hurt again but she was effectively setting herself up for possibly the biggest fall of her life. Not even the horrific, frantic pace of a war zone could block out the pain he could cause if he rejected her love.

She took a breath. 'I take it you didn't run into any problems on your drive home?'

'No. You're a little later than I expected.'

'When did you expect me?'

'At least five minutes ago.'

'That's not a little later, that's five minutes, you *oie-tête*.'

He chuckled. 'What did you just call me?'

'Goose-head.'

'What on earth is that supposed to be? No, wait. Don't bother. I don't think I want to know.'

Nicolette joined in his laughter, her earlier apprehension gone. It had been replaced by a warm, secure feeling that Stephen didn't want to keep their relationship strictly business.

'It's nothing bad. Just a silly childhood name my brothers and I used to call each other.'

'So long as it's nothing bad, then.'

Both were silent for a moment, their laughter dying away.

'*Bonne nuit*, Nicolette.' His voice was soft and gentle as he told her to have sweet dreams.

'*A toi aussi.*' She disconnected the call and whispered into the dark, '*Mon chéri.*'

At three o'clock, she began to think sleep would never claim her. Stephen had told her to have sweet dreams and that would be good if she could only settle her mind.

What did he want to discuss with her? Three thousand different scenarios had filtered through her head...well, perhaps no more than ten but it certainly felt like three thousand and her brain was just refusing to switch off and go to sleep.

All she wanted to do was lie there and dream about Stephen. The tender way he touched her hand, the way his lips brushed hers, tantalising and teasing her before the fierceness of their attraction took over. The way his body felt so perfect pressed against her own.

At five-thirty she gave up all pretence, deciding it was better to shower and dress and hopefully get some work done. It was then she recalled that she didn't have any work to do. As Dr River had left the majority of the case load to her, she'd often brought casenotes home so she could either research, study or just write up what had happened with the patient in question. Now, though, working in a practice where the other doctor actually carried his weight, she found she didn't have any extra paperwork to do. It was quite a strange feeling.

'I'll read a book,' she decided firmly. It had been ages since she'd had the time to indulge in reading, and excitedly picked up the book Luc had sent for her birthday over six months ago. At first she read the same page over and over, her mind still refusing to be distracted, but after persisting she managed to snuggle up in front of the fire and read. At seven o'clock she fell asleep and woke just before nine with a stiff neck.

'That'll teach you,' she muttered crossly as she massaged her neck. Her head felt as though it was full of cotton wool and she needed to get outside to clear the stuffiness.

She tugged on warm socks and her walking boots before pulling on her coat and woollen hat. She wound her scarf around her neck and picked up her keys and gloves. After shutting the door, she let the cold morning air hit her and welcomed its freshness.

Her favourite walk to Bridal Veil Falls wasn't far and she set off, sliding her fingers into her gloves and then shoving her hands deep into the pockets of her coat. It was cold, it was brisk but it was just what she needed.

Nicolette was determined to enjoy the walk as she always did, and forced herself to take in her surroundings rather than dwell on Stephen…but she found herself failing quite often. She longed to bring him here, knowing he would love the place. Perhaps he'd want to paint it and perhaps he'd let her watch. She was curious about his painting and wondered if he'd ever let her see her work.

She waltzed through the car park and headed down the steps to the falls below. It was a popular destination and the car park was big enough for several tourist buses to park and turn around. Nicolette was just thankful the tourists hadn't yet arrived for the day.

A few steps from the base of the falls she saw someone up ahead. She slowed her pace, not wanting to disturb them. Through the foliage, she realised the person was sitting down…painting. Warmth flooded through her in the hope that it was Stephen. Was he a morning person? Was that when he did his painting? There was still so much she needed to know about him.

On tenterhooks, she crept closer, not wanting to disturb the man but wanting to see if it was Stephen.

It was!

Her heart thudded so wildly against her chest she thought she'd wake any sleeping wildlife around. The birds were all awake and singing their beautiful songs and so, too, were her heart and mind. She shifted off the path to head towards him. A twig snapped underfoot and she looked up, expecting him to turn and see her, but instead he continued to paint.

Nicolette smiled. It was then she realised he had headphones on and she could now hear the muffled beat of heavy rock. How on earth could he create with such noise blaring in his head?

Then she looked at the canvas. This was obviously not his first trip here as the painting was well and truly established, but she gasped at what she saw.

The background held the natural beauty and splendour of Bridal Veil Falls cascading down over the rocks. The native trees were painted perfectly but it was the person in the painting that made her gasp. On one of the rocks in the middle of the pool was a woman. A woman who had blonde hair and brown eyes.

A woman whose face smiled back at her from the mirror every time she looked into it.

Stephen had painted her into the picture! But why?

It was then he turned and saw her. He froze for a few heart-stopping moments before he pulled the headphones from his ears, his gaze never leaving hers. 'Good morning.'

'I'm in that painting.' There was going to be no small talk. She had too many questions that needed answers.

'Yes.' Still no movement.

'Why?'

'Because I'm trying to paint you out.' His gaze was steady on hers as he spoke, his words causing hope to come more strongly to life.

'Why?'

Stephen exhaled slowly and finally stood. He came over and stood next to her, viewing his painting critically. 'It's not too bad but I don't think I'll ever be able to com-

pletely capture all the colours in your hair. It's so...
sensual. It's hard to paint sensual.'

Nicolette swallowed over her dry throat. 'I think you've
done an amazing job. She looks just like me.'

'Thank you.'

She turned to face him. 'But why, Stephen? Why the
need to paint me at all?'

Stephen shifted so he could see her better, and gazed
longingly into her warm brown eyes. 'Don't you have any
idea what you do to me?'

She paused, her heart swelling with love for him. 'I
need you to tell me.'

'Tell you what? That I can't stop thinking about you?
That even when I try to relax by painting, you somehow
find your way onto the canvas? I thought at first I could
paint you out, but the more I tried, the more I failed.
You've stayed, Nicolette, and that has scared me, and it
takes a lot to scare me.'

The smile on her face was one of pure love and she
hoped it shone through, that he could not only see how
much she needed him but also felt how special he was to
her. 'I know the feeling.'

'Do you? And what do you do about it?' His tone was
earnest and clear.

'I don't fight it. I haven't fought it for quite some time
now and I've found that helps.'

'Stop fighting?'

'Yes.'

'That would mean I have to tell you how much I love
you.'

Nicolette gasped, her bottom lip quivering and her eyes
beginning to fill with tears. She brushed them away impatiently, not wanting anything to blur her vision at this
most life-changing moment.

'Yes,' she whispered. 'Yes, it would.'

'By declaring my love, it means I've opened myself up to the possibility of hurt.'

'Yes…but I could never hurt you.' She pulled off her gloves and reached out, caressing his cheek. 'I love you too much to do that.' He sucked in a deep breath and took her hand in his, tugging her closer until his arms could close around her.

'You love me?' He was stunned and she laughed at his disbelief.

'How can you doubt it?' A teasing glint entered her eyes. 'Let me prove it to you.' She pressed little kisses to his neck. *'Tu es adorable…'* More kisses across the lower part of his jaw. *'Et sexy…'* A kiss on the corners of his mouth. *'Et complètement chaud pour moi.'*

'Really?' He raised his eyebrows.

'Oui.'

'I'm hot for you?'

'Oui.'

He gathered her as close as he could, given their bulky clothing, and nuzzled her ear lobe. 'Mmm. I guess you're right. Despite it being a cold morning, I am toasty-roasty, basking in the unbelievable knowledge that you love me.'

'If you don't hurry up and kiss me, I won't be held accountable for my actions.'

'But you said you'd never hurt me,' he reminded her.

'Never intentionally, but isn't it hurting you *not* to kiss me?'

'Sweet torture,' he murmured as he took a turn to press kisses to her neck. *'Tu es belle…'* He worked his way around to her lips. *'Tu es intelligente.'*

'Will you hurry up?'

He lifted his head and smiled down into her beautiful face. *'Oui, ma chérie.'*

Finally, his lips found hers and although both were eager to renew their acquaintance, there was also something very different in this kiss compared to the others they'd shared. This one declared the emotions they were both feeling, were understood and returned, as well as being for life.

The ringing of a phone pierced the stillness around them and Nicolette jumped.

Stephen smiled as he shifted slightly, not at all inclined to let go of the woman who meant everything to him, and pulled his phone from his pocket. 'That'll be Steph.' He answered the call. 'Hey, sis. How's Sydney?'

'What's going on? I hardly slept last night and have been feeling quite miserable, and then a few minutes ago everything lifted and I can't stop smiling!'

'Is she *feeling* you again?' Nicolette complained loudly.

'Nic's with you?'

'Yes.'

'And you're *happy*?' Stephanie fished.

'Extremely.'

A piercing scream came from his sister and he held the phone away from his ear, both of them laughing. He took the opportunity to press a few more kisses to Nicolette's lips before returning his attention to his sister.

'So are you getting married?'

'Am I getting married? Well, I don't know. I haven't had a chance to ask her yet so give me a moment and I'll fix it.' He put the phone down on the ground and dropped to one knee, taking both Nicolette's hands in his. She gasped with delight.

'Nicolette, we may not have known each other long, but we've got to know each other more deeply than I've ever known a woman before. You are vitally important to me and I want you with me. Not only in business but in my personal life, too. Stephanie told me the mountains would help me find my smile again but, although they've helped, it's been you who's performed that miracle. You understand me and you're on my wavelength. You are everything to me and I want you with me for ever. Please.' He squeezed her hand. 'Be my wife?'

Nicolette dropped down on one knee also, facing him, letting him see just how much she loved him. 'There's no longer any need for pretence, no need to hide how much you mean to me. I love you with every fibre of my being and I would love to be your wife, to make a life with you, to have children with you, to work with you, to encourage and support you. You are my equal, Stephen, the other half of me, and I am so glad I've finally found you.'

Tears were sliding down her cheeks as she spoke, her words choking in her throat due to the intensity of her emotion, but he heard every word and it took a few microseconds for it all to sink in. She loved him! He still couldn't believe it, but what she'd said had been correct—they were each other's missing halves, and together they made a whole.

The screaming from the telephone on the ground startled them both. Laughing, he picked up the phone. 'Happy now?'

'Yes. Let me speak to Nic.' Stephen handed the phone across. 'Nic, I've always loved you like a sister from the moment we met, and now you really are going to be my sister. Thank you for respecting the bond Stephen and I have and for letting me be a part of such an intimate and private moment.'

Nicolette smiled. 'What are sisters for? Have fun in Sydney. I'll be expecting a *full* debrief—and I mean *full*—later on in the week.'

Stephanie just laughed as Nicolette handed the phone

back to Stephen. 'I'll call you later. Be safe.' He ended the call and pocketed the phone before drawing Nicolette up with him. 'I love you,' he said again, pulling her into his arms. 'Let me pack up my gear so we can get out of here. Now that I don't have to worry about luring you to my home under false pretences, I can hardly wait to actually hold you without all this extra padding.'

Nicolette laughed, happier than she'd ever been in her life.

Stephen cupped her face in his hands and pressed his lips to hers with absolute wonderment and conviction. Finally, he'd found the place where he belonged and it was here, in Nicolette's arms.

'So do we need to discuss business or is this a real *date*?' she couldn't help teasing.

'No business,' he declared emphatically. 'Definitely *no* business.'

'Then it's a date.'

MILLS & BOON®

Live the emotion

_MedicaL
romance™

THE CELEBRITY DOCTOR'S PROPOSAL

by Sarah Morgan

When Dr Sam McKenna left his home town, he landed a prime-time TV slot. *Medical Matters* is top of the ratings! Now Sam has been roped in to be GP Anna Riggs's locum for the summer – and he's dragged his film crew along with him! Anna's furious – but then she realises that Sam's caring attitude is not simply a camera trick!

UNDERCOVER AT CITY HOSPITAL

by Carol Marinelli (Police Surgeons)

Sexy ER consultant Heath Jameson catches Bella's eye instantly – but she knows she shouldn't get involved. She is a police officer, working undercover in the hospital to catch a drug thief, and she can't risk exposing her investigation. But Bella can still feel her life beginning to change, no matter how hard she tries to resist their mutual attraction…

A MOTHER FOR HIS FAMILY *by Alison Roberts*

Nurse Sarah Mitchell wants to relax on her Fijian holiday. The last thing she wants is a fling with playboy Dr Ben Dawson. Until a cyclone hits the tropics and Sarah sees the true Ben – a talented surgeon with a big heart, a past, and a daughter in need of TLC. But Ben's attempts at love have hurt him before – can he trust his instincts again?

On sale 1st July 2005

Available at most branches of WHSmith, Tesco, ASDA, Martins, Borders, Eason, Sainsbury's and all good paperback bookshops.

Visit www.millsandboon.co.uk

MILLS & BOON®

0605/03b

Live the emotion

_Medical romance™

A SPECIAL KIND OF CARING by Jennifer Taylor

Dr Francesca Goodwin wants to escape – from London, from the pain of her last relationship, from people. Working as a GP in isolated Teesdale sounds perfect – until she meets her new partner, Dr Alex Shepherd. He's good-looking, caring – and attracted to her!

THE FLIGHT DOCTOR'S LIFELINE by Laura Iding

(Air Rescue)

Helicopter pilot Reese Jarvis is drawn to Dr Samantha Kearn from the moment he sees her in action with the Lifeline Medical Air Transport team. When he learns she is having trouble with her ex-husband, he immediately wants to protect her. He becomes her lifeline, her support – but ever since his fiancée died he has been reluctant to put his feelings on the line…

THE BUSH DOCTOR'S RESCUE by Leah Martyn

Nurse Ally Inglis doesn't know why Dr Marc Ballantyne has come to the Outback town of Hillcrest, she's just grateful to have a full-time doctor at last. Marc charms and surprises everyone – not least of all Ally. He stirs up feelings she thought she'd never have again. But she can't help wondering, does this modern-day knight *really* mean to rescue her heart…?

On sale 1st July 2005

Available at most branches of WHSmith, Tesco, ASDA, Martins, Borders, Eason, Sainsbury's and all good paperback bookshops.

Visit www.millsandboon.co.uk

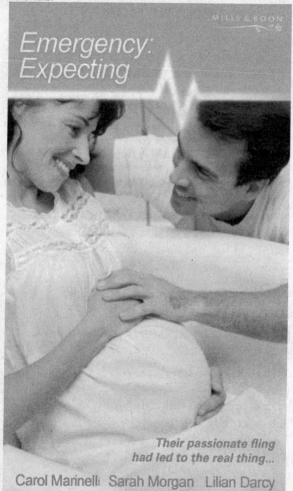

On sale 1st July 2005

*Available at most branches of WHSmith, Tesco, ASDA, Martins,
Borders, Eason, Sainsbury's and all good paperback bookshops.*

FREE!

4 Books
and a surprise gift!

We would like to take this opportunity to thank you for reading this Mills & Boon® book by offering you the chance to take FOUR more specially selected titles from the Medical Romance™ series absolutely FREE! We're also making this offer to introduce you to the benefits of the Reader Service™—

- ★ FREE home delivery
- ★ FREE gifts and competitions
- ★ FREE monthly Newsletter
- ★ Exclusive Reader Service offers
- ★ Books available before they're in the shops

Accepting these FREE books and gift places you under no obligation to buy, you may cancel at any time, even after receiving your free shipment. Simply complete your details below and return the entire page to the address below. You don't even need a stamp!

YES! Please send me 4 free Medical Romance books and a surprise gift. I understand that unless you hear from me, I will receive 6 superb new titles every month for just £2.75 each, postage and packing free. I am under no obligation to purchase any books and may cancel my subscription at any time. The free books and gift will be mine to keep in any case.

M5ZEF

Ms/Mrs/Miss/Mr ....Initials ....
BLOCK CAPITALS PLEASE

Surname ....

Address...

....

....Postcode ....

Send this whole page to:
UK: FREEPOST CN81, Croydon, CR9 3WZ